HDQ

D0399398

DATE DUE		10/01
NOV 2 7 01		
DEC 2 6 01		
JAN 2 4 02		
2/7/02		
MAR 30 02		
APR 1 5 02		
OCT 1 1 01		
FEB 2 8 04		
GAYLORD		PRINTED IN U.S.A.

Creatures
of Habit

Also by Jill McCorkle

Creatures
of Habit

❧ *STORIES* ❧

JILL MCCORKLE

Algonquin Books
of Chapel Hill

2001

JACKSON COUNTY LIBRARY SERVICES
MEDFORD OREGON 97501

R

A SHANNON RAVENEL BOOK
Published by
Algonquin Books of Chapel Hill
Post Office Box 2225
Chapel Hill, North Carolina 27515-2225

a division of
Workman Publishing
708 Broadway
New York, New York 10003

© 2001 by Jill McCorkle. All rights reserved.
Printed in the United States of America.
Published simultaneously in Canada
by Thomas Allen & Son Limited.
Design by Anne Winslow.

Some of the stories here originally appeared with different titles and in slightly different versions in the following magazines and anthologies, to whose editors grateful acknowledgment is made: "Snipe" appeared as "The Snipe Hunt" in *Off the Beaten Path*, published by The Nature Conservancy/Northpoint Press, 1998; "Dogs" appeared as "Mad Dogs" in the *Boston Globe* Summer Fiction Issue, 2000; and "Toads" appeared as "Fake Man" in *Epoch* (Volume 48, Number 3).

This is a work of fiction. While, as in all fiction, the literary perceptions and insights are based on experience, all names, characters, places, and incidents are either products of the author's imagination or are used fictiously. No reference to any real person is intended or should be inferred.

Library of Congress Cataloging-in-Publication Data
McCorkle, Jill, 1958–
    Creatures of habit : stories / by Jill McCorkle.
        p. cm.
    ISBN 1-56512-256-9 (hardcover)
    1. North Carolina—Social life and customs—Fiction. 2. Human-animal relationships—Fiction. 3. Animals—Fiction. I. Title.
PS3563.C3444 C74 2001
813'.54—dc21   2001034835

10 9 8 7 6 5 4 3 2 1
First Edition

JACKSON COUNTY LIBRARY SERVICES
MEDFORD OREGON 97501

For my family
then and now, always and forever

A grateful thanks to friends who read these stories in their earlier forms. And eternal thanks to A.H. for a room of my own.

When movements, associated through habits with certain states of the mind, are partially repressed by the will, the strictly involuntary muscles, as well as those which are least under the separate control of the will, are liable still to act; and their action is often highly expressive.

Charles Darwin
The Expression of the Emotions in Man and Animals

Contents

Creatures
of Habit

Billy Goats

WE USED TO all come outside when the streetlights came on and prowl the neighborhood in a pack, a herd of kids on banana-seat bikes and minibikes. The grown-ups looked so silly framed in their living-room and kitchen windows. They complained about their days and sighed deep sighs of depression and loss. They talked about how spoiled and lucky children were these days. *We will never be that way, we said, we will never say those things.* We popped wheelies in pursuit of the mosquito truck, which was a guarantee on humid summer nights. We rode behind the big gray truck, our laughter and screams lost in the grinding whir of machinery, our vision blurred by the cloud of poison. We were light-headed as we cruised our town—the dark deserted playground of the elementary school, the fluorescent-lit gas stations out on the service road of the interstate that scarred the rural landscape, past the run-down apartment complex where transient military families lived, past houses that were identified by histories of death, divorce, disaster. Sometimes we rode up to the hospital, a three-story red brick building that stayed lit throughout the night. We hid in the shrubbery of what was known as the lawyers' parking lot, a spot near the courthouse rumored to be the scene of many late-night rendezvous between people you would be shocked to see—mothers and fathers you would never suspect doing such things while their spouses and children lay asleep in their beds.

We rode way out past the tobacco warehouses and the railroad tracks, past the small footbridge where we used to play billy goats Gruff, our idea of who was scary enough to be the troll ever changing. We rode on, out to the local kennel, where one imitation bark could set off a satisfying round of howls that continued long after we'd ridden off in the direction of Bell's Econo Lodge, where we slipped fully clothed into the warm green water of the fenced-in pool, our cutoffs and T-shirts weighing us down as we bobbed and paddled back and forth. Sometimes we just floated there, buoyed by the constant rush of cars on the interstate and the still patterns of stars overhead.

One night we stopped and sat in a circle under the streetlight on my corner. We avoided the gaping storm drain across from us, home of many lost baseballs and bracelets and shoes. Only a few of us had ever been brave enough to go down into the dark muddy box in search of lost items. Those who did surfaced with vows never to do it again. This night we talked about *Laugh-In* and took turns imitating the stars: "sock it to me" and "one ringy dingy" and "verrry interesting." One boy, tall with a freckled complexion and ears that stuck out from his head, was a bit of an outcast at the junior high school. But here in the neighborhood where he had lived his entire life, he fit in. This night, he told how he had ridden his bike to the emergency room earlier in the day and seen a woman whose face was torn away, a child with a broken leg that dangled from its hip like a bruised banana, another woman who had tried to kill herself on aspirin and failed. He said he heard them pump her stomach. He heard her vomiting and begging to die behind a curtain meant for children patients, its little farm animals in primary colors swaying back and forth with the movement of the tall oscillating fan in the corner. "It was so weird," he told all of us, who hung on his every word. "The incongruity of it all." His acute observations and large vocabulary that brought laughter and scorn in the classroom were accepted—really expected—by the neighborhood crowd. We counted on him to bring us the kind of news that left us weak in the knees and too nervous to sleep.

One girl was planning to stay out this whole night. Her parents were out of town and her older brother didn't give a damn what she did as long as she didn't tell that his girlfriend was going to sleep upstairs in his lower bunk. If she wanted to, she could smoke cigarettes and rummage through her parents' drawers for signs of their sex life. She could drink some wine and watch TV all night, go door-to-door at dawn stealing the milk and the Krispy Kreme doughnuts that were delivered to doorsteps.

We talked that night, as usual, about the murder-suicide house, which was just two blocks away, a tidy brick colonial with a bricked-in herb garden—long untended—complete with a sundial. Some nights we dared to creep into the yard and collect sprigs of mint and lavender that we would rub and sniff for a long time after. We knew all the details of the house's story even though everything had happened a whole generation before when our parents were growing up here. There was the murdered woman, an accomplished violinist.

It had been her desire to teach the violin, but when there was no real interest in town (who, after all, actually owned a violin?), she taught voice and piano lessons. There was her husband, the suicide man, who had once lived in Chicago, a detail that was always included to mark him as an outsider no matter how many years he had lived in town. There was their one son, who came back from his home in California to bury them both in an expensive mausoleum at the center of Hollydale Cemetery. Before the son left town, never to be heard from again, he told people that his parents had made a suicide pact. We were left wondering which was worse: to have one parent a murderer or to have both parents choose to depart this earth without a thought about how it might affect your life? Theirs were not the only suicides in our town; there were more than we would ever have guessed, but we took turns telling what we knew about reported hunting accidents and accidental overdoses, whispering as if the deceased might suddenly step from the thick pine woods behind us.

We also talked about the famous Hank Carter, said to have been a genius who "crossed the line." None of the parents explained exactly what the line was or how crossing it happened or if there were warning signs. All we knew was that Hank was proof you could go from being a clean, well-dressed high-school student who solved difficult calculus problems and aspired to be a NASA engineer to being a disheveled, bearded man who wore a cowboy hat and boots and rode around on a moped with a pistol and other weaponry attached to his belt and a Bible tied to the handlebars. Sometimes Hank threatened to shoot dogs and cats and the tires of expensive cars, and other times he preached, though no church in town had ever claimed him as one of its own.

We were discussing it all this night in July 1970, the summer of the Jeffrey MacDonald hearing. Jeffrey MacDonald was the man charged with murdering his whole family—two little girls and a pregnant wife—on the army base nearby. He claimed to have seen a band of hippies enter his darkened home. He said he heard them saying things like *acid is groovy* and *kill the pigs* just before performing an atrocious re-enactment of the Manson family murders. It had happened back in February and it was what the grown-ups discussed over their highballs and cigarettes, coffee and Jell-O, and Saturday night T-bones ever since. Had this good-looking surgeon, brilliant enough to have gone to Princeton, really butchered his young family? Was it possible that someone so smart and skillful could lose his mind, just snap and go into a bloodbath frenzy? To tell the truth, many kids had not slept through a night since February. Our minds were full of images of the beautiful young and blonde Mrs. MacDonald and of her babies and with the bits of gory detail the adults stopped describing whenever we passed through a room.

"My God," the tall freckled boy said. "Like we don't read the newspapers, too." And then he recited newspaper accounts of the state of the bodies, leaving us more light-headed than the mosquito truck had.

"Hank Carter has crossed over; he might snap even more," one of us inevitably said, and though the whole town had proclaimed Hank harmless, there being no reports whatsoever of his ever hurting any person or pet, I could never look him in the eye, even when he yelled in a booming, slow-as-molasses voice, "I say, girl, have you got the correct eastern standard time?"

Back then, when I wanted the time, I went to the phone and dialed 739-3241 and a man would say *The correct time is eight-oh-two* PM *and forty seconds*. I must have called him twenty times a day. He became a security blanket of sorts. Even now, almost thirty years later, I can close my eyes and hear every beat of his mechanical voice.

WE WERE TOO old for kick the can and too young to make out. We were restless. We had learned a lot about murder that year. We knew that most of the time a person knows the person killing them. We had learned that alcohol and cigarettes would begin to kill off people we loved. Some of the grown-ups who sheltered us were disappearing from their windows like fade-outs, images lifted from the earth in poofs of smoke, puddles of drink. We were learning that, to be lost, a brain didn't have to be blown out all over a ceiling like in the murder-suicide house at the edge of town. We knew people whose brains were slipping down a long easy slope. There was a teacher we loved who got us confused with our parents. There was a man well loved in town for entertaining at children's birthday parties (a mediocre magician with an aging pet monkey) who had ended his own life.

"He was queer," said some older boys who had taken to hanging out in our neighborhood. "He was an old cocksucker." These were the same older boys who, one dark night that very summer, forced the freckle-faced boy to go down on them and then told us about it. They called him queer and they called him cocksucker and it didn't seem to occur to them that they were the ones who had demanded the act of him, that they were the ones who had pulled his serious young face into their damp bitter crotches and issued their orders. Did it occur to us?

So WE DID have to wonder about death. The slow poisoning of lungs and livers and brains. The pact a couple might make to end it all. The savage stabbing a man might fly off and commit. A kid—never the hunter, always the prey—whose only crime was that he was scared and too tired to fight back and who, when he could no longer live with the pressure building up in his mind, chose to treat himself with a gun barrel forced down his throat. But the boys who promised to share a beer with him out in the dark woods near the highway probably didn't make that connection. They probably grew up to drink their own highballs while their own children played outdoors, riding their bikes past the latest sites of domestic unrest.

As grown-ups, you have to stop and wonder what people are thinking, or not thinking. Do those boys, grown into the bodies of men, carry that death around in their pockets? Do they ever, at the height of sexual climax, see that boy there, his sad eyes pleading *Let me go*?

And the suicide-pact story, who knows if it was true? There was the note the son found, but how do we know the son didn't write it himself as a way to protect his dead parents? Or maybe the husband wrote it after he killed her. Maybe it was a murder of hatred, a murder of passion, and then he left behind a legacy of mutual love and decision. We will never know.

THERE WAS ANOTHER house in town, a beautiful Victorian with a little circular tower. It was surrounded by an ornate fence, each iron picket the shape of an arrow. I loved the house and its fence until I heard that there had once been a terrible car crash on the corner. A young passenger, a boy, was thrown through the windshield and onto those iron arrows. It had happened twenty years earlier when my parents were teenagers, back when the interstate didn't exist, back when people didn't know the danger of smoking the very tobacco that so many had helped to harvest. I tried to get the image of the speared boy out of my mind, but I was never able to pass that house without seeing him pinned there under the blue sky of a beautiful October afternoon.

That image, and the one of the middle-aged woman, violin in hand, son living elsewhere, begging for her life, hang on in my imagination. Sometimes the violinist's face gets confused with that of Mrs. Colette MacDonald. The stories of one person begging, another taking, run parallel.

It is said the MacDonald house remained vacant and untouched for years. The food in the freezer, the valentines out on display. I could not imagine my father in such a fit of rage, but some of my friends said they could imagine theirs that way. Some kids had seen their parents drunk. All of us had overheard at least one really bad argument. Most of us had seen our parents cry, and even for those who glimpsed only the briefest losses of control, the memories remained vivid. Our parents were as vulnerable as we were. Anyone, grown-ups and children alike, could die at any minute. They could disappear as quickly as a car crashed into a tree, or a trigger was pulled, an overdose or undetected cancer cell flowed through the bloodstream; their hearts, livers, or lungs might shut down, some with warnings, others without.

We all had experienced the desire for breath, the burning ache of our lungs when we shot up from the deep end of the motel pool to the surface of light and gasped for air, when we tumbled from our bikes, dizzy and high, to roll in someone's front yard and spit out the taste of mosquito poison. The wonder of that first full breath. Jeffrey MacDonald claimed in his trial to have given mouth-to-mouth to his wife. He claimed that he could hear the breath exit through her chest as quickly as he delivered it. Too late.

THE LAST TIME I ever saw Hank Carter he was directing traffic around an accident at an intersection near the high school. We all stopped to watch him there, cowboy hat pulled low, beard long and unkempt, billy stick swinging from his belt. He wore some mirrored sunglasses and moved quickly, pushing bystanders over toward the curb as he tried to make the two men involved in the fender bender sit down and breathe into paper bags. When he was dismissed from his post by a policeman, he reluctantly returned to his motorbike, which a crowd of us stood around. It was old and rusty. Ropes, flashlights, and fast-food bags were crammed in the basket on the back along with the Bible, yellowed and swollen from exposure to the weather.

"What's doin' Hank?" one of the boys yelled in a slow mimic. "Shot anything lately?" Traffic was moving by then and we were ready to move on ourselves. We were in high school. We had afternoon jobs and study dates. We had a prom to plan and decorate.

"Nothin' but some old mean blue jays," he called back, mounting his bike like it was a horse. "There weren't nothin' left but a few feathers and some bird gut." He pulled a blue feather from his back pocket and waved it back and forth, laughing until he began to cough and wheeze, a cigarette burning to ash between two fingers of his waving hand.

The boys liked to keep Hank talking. They liked to get him riled up over some topic far removed from the moment. They wanted his ranting and raving but not directed

at them. It was a fine line they walked; a minefield of topics guaranteed to set him off. He hated dogs that barked
when he rode past them. He'd like to see their vocal chords
tied up into knots. That would leave them silent. "I hate a
damn barking dog," he said. "I hate 'em like I hate a Com-
munist. I'd shoot me some dog if the law would allow it.
They should've let me loose in Vietnam." He didn't believe
that men had gone to the moon. He said all that stuff was
filmed right down near the coast. "Down where you girls
strip naked and grease your bodies to get that tan. The Lord
would not like that." He laughed and shook his head. "The
Lord would not like that one damn bit." He thought that
women should not be allowed to drive cars, especially the
really young women and the really old women and the foreign women. "A woman is good for one thing," he said, and
the boys egged him on. "Not for *cooking*," he said, and ad-
justed his mirrored sunglasses that made it hard to know
what he was staring at. "Though I'd not turn myself down
a meal of fried chicken and mashed potatoes. Don't need
one for cleaning, neither," he said. "I can operate me a
Hoover as good as any old woman. Got me a Hoover so
goddamned powerful I can use it to rake up yards if I take a
notion."

"So, you got yourself a woman, Hank?" one of the boys

asked. Asking this kind of question was like playing Russian roulette. He might laugh but he was just as likely to fire his pistol into the air and command some *goddamn* respect for the weaker sex. He often preached about Adam and Eve, which was exactly what the boys were hoping for. He could go on for hours about how that naked harlot was put there in the garden for one thing and one thing only until she took up with that devil snake and got it in her evil mind that she wanted herself some knowledge other than making some babies to populate the earth. "She was nothing but a rib," he said, "and Adam had every right to kick her ass." He said, "The great and almighty plan was not supposed to take such a turn."

Everyone knew that as a high school student he had dated Emma Mosby, a girl who grew up to marry another town boy, one who went off to school and then to the Korean War and then back to school and became a surgeon and then chief of staff at the hospital. They lived in an old house in the center of town, a block Hank circled endlessly. He was dating Emma Mosby when he began to cross over. One day he was telling her how much he loved her and explaining how suspension bridges are built and the very next week he arrived at her house suited up like someone going to a rodeo and complained of all the racket the dogs were making, those cussing belligerent damned dogs. Emma Mosby's time in love with Hank Carter was something that everyone knew about but no one discussed. "Emma doesn't deserve to have that dredged up," the grown-ups would say.

But the day at the accident was the last time I ever saw him. The boys hoped for an angry answer but Hank just shook his head and laughed. "For me to know and you to find out," he said. "You find out and I'm likely to reward you with a dollar bill or two." He mounted his bike and the group cleared a path for him.

"Hey there, girl," he drawled when he saw me standing there. "Do I know you?" He lifted his sunglasses to reveal clear blue, much-younger-looking eyes than I would ever have expected. "Are you the one been calling up to my house and hanging up? Or asking is my Frigidaire running or have I got Prince Albert in the can?" I shook my head, my face hot. I wanted to look away from him but I was afraid of making him mad.

"Not me," I said, while a chorus of boys behind me sang out things like *Yeah right. Sure. You want us to believe that?*

"If that's what she says then that's what she means, you bunch of stupid boys." He turned on them then, patted the big gun strapped to his hip. "You all look like a pack of mean

old junkyard dogs to me. Damn Nazi mongrels." Everyone
froze while he twirled his gun and then eased it back into
the holster on his belt, alongside his big silver flashlight
and the billy stick. "The good Lord hates the Nazis and the
Commies and the ignoramuses, and I've been put here to
keep a watch. Ain't nobody gettin' by me." He laughed his
loud laugh and then turned back to me. "I've known you
forever, girl," he said. "I know your whole life like a book. I
always have and I always will." He shook his head and
dropped his glasses back in place. "Don't you ever forget
that." He made a clicking sound from the corner of his
mouth, the kind of sound that someone might use to ac-
company a wink, though now his pale blue young eyes were
hidden again. I nodded. No one spoke until he cranked his
bike and rode well past the intersection as he headed out toward the service road.

I WAS A SENIOR in college when I got word that
Hank Carter had died. I was two hours and light-years away;
I was in a place where my memories were something I could
bend and shape into a suitable representation of who I was. I
hung out at an old house at the edge of campus where there
was always a gathering of students listening to music and

drinking beer, discussing philosophy and religion and the fate of the world. My hometown paper said Hank died of a heart attack. Those among the huge outpouring of viewers said he looked small lying in his coffin without his hat and boots, his face shaved smooth. They said he looked like a normal person. Receding hairline. Wrinkles around his eyes and on his pale white throat that had always been protected by a red bandanna and the scraggly beard. They said he died at twelve noon, and for several months after that, when the bell of the Methodist church chimed the hour, people would pause over their lunches to comment how they missed seeing Hank riding through town. Until he died, they hadn't taken into account how many times a week they saw him— helping at accidents or collecting litter along the highway or just riding his motorbike through town.

As a child, I had a contest with myself to see how many times I could call the time service before the minute lapsed. It was a reassuring thing to do. And now other numbers I called often crowd my mind like secret codes: 3642 and 5756. If I could be in a *Twilight Zone* episode, it would be the one where the phone line has fallen down onto a grave so that calls are placed from beyond. If I could write my own episode, it would involve a phone line that could connect us back to those old places. Just dial and you get your grandfather in his wheelchair, his tired old collie curled beside him; your grandmother in her kitchen with Mason jars sterilized and ready to receive tomatoes and pear preserves; the neighbor saving her mail so when you got home from kindergarten you could use her jewel-handled letter opener —razor sharp—to slit the white envelopes of her bills and the pale ones of letters; the old aunt who kept a jar of peppermints for children and who always spoke with her hand covering poor dental work, her head tilted just slightly; fathers walking up from the eighteenth hole on late Sunday afternoons while mothers bundled their children into big warm towels as they stepped from the pool, eyes red and stinging from the chlorine; the freckle-faced boy, waiting on his bike, ready to race through the summer night with the sound of an ambulance on the highway. *Won't one of you please, please, please go with me?*

I WOULD CALL the people I knew growing up who have since died. I would ask how life had taken them there. Did they beg or did they pass in silence? Did they embrace life or reject it? Were there memories that at the very last minute filled their minds and swaddled their fears? And like a director, I would call for lights to come on in every house in town and for every person who had ever lived there to step outside and take a long deep breath on this average summer night.

Snipe

CAROLINE AND HER brother stood in the darkness of the woods. They held a big burlap sack between them and watched their father disappear down the path back to the house. Though the lights from the house were hidden by the slope of the hill and the thick dark pine branches, Caroline knew that she was still within yelling distance, and now she had that impulse. "Daddy!" she called, her high-pitched voice interrupting the incessant drone of crickets. She ignored Danny's elbow digging into her hip to silence her. "Daddy, where are you?"

"Hush up," Danny said and she knew his teeth were gritted though she could barely make out the profile of his thin face. "We ain't gonna catch nothing if you act like this."

Caroline quieted with Danny's words as she usually did. After all, he was older; he was going to be in the fourth grade come fall and she would be starting school for the very first time. The thought of first grade and the stories about how the principal carried a big paddle through the halls burned through her body like comets, causing her to wake up at night all that summer to either a wet bed or a dizzy feeling as if she had been spun around and around like a June bug on a string.

"The principal is a wonderful man," her mother would say, but Danny—at the table, in a doorway, beside her in the backseat of the old blue Rambler—would glance down with raised eyebrows, shake his head, sigh, and her mother's soothing words would fly past like Roman candles shot into the sky.

"I'll watch out for you at school if you do whatever I say," Danny had told her with such forceful authority that she was able to go for thirty-minute stretches without worrying about it all. "You know, like if I hear you've disappeared from first grade, I'll go down to that dungeon where he puts the bad children, and I'll spring you."

But now in the prickly darkness of the woods, even with him there beside her, the fears came back. What if they did catch a snipe? What if one of those huge brown birds all of the relatives talked about did fly from the woods to the hole in their big burlap sack? Caroline braced herself, determined not to scream when it happened, determined not to be a baby. Danny was already mad at her; he was mad at everybody and had been all day long.

She listened for her father's and Uncle Tim's footsteps but all she heard was the frogs and crickets. She tried to think about how she had felt earlier in the afternoon and the excitement of waiting for the relatives to arrive. The kitchen table was covered with food, big watermelons cooled on the back porch, and the box of fireworks that had been on a high shelf was down where she could see into it. But not touch them. Not even Danny could touch them.

THE RELATIVES HAD arrived for the Fourth of July —"descended like a swarm of locusts," Caroline's mother whispered—their paneled station wagon so loaded down with bodies and watermelons and Tupperware that it scraped its bottom coming up the drive.

Caroline was straddling the porch banister, holding a piece of twine tied around the post like reins, when they arrived. She had spent most of the day at the town pool and her eyes were burning. The whole world was a blur. The porch began to vibrate with music from the living room, where the three teenage cousins immediately huddled around the record player. One of them had her hair rolled up around orange-juice cans. Two others, Uncle Tim and Aunt Patricia's daughters, had arrived with little round carrying cases filled with records. They sang "Where the Boys Are" and argued over who was the best-looking doctor, Ben Casey or Dr. Kildare. They marveled at the fact that Caroline's mother had a record of "Moon River" and a Chubby Checker album, which the one in braces said was her "fave." They argued over what was the best way to tease hair and then they whispered about Mark Eden and laughed. Caroline was taking notes in her head. This was her assignment: Hear all you can but don't say one word, not to anybody. She knew that somewhere out in the yard Danny was hiding and watching to make sure she passed the test. If she passed today, he would let her go to the pool with him again tomorrow and he would even admit to people that she was his sister. Today she had been an orphaned neighbor child he was being paid big money to watch.

Next door, Mrs. Hopper was stretched out in her lounge chair even though it was after four. Her sprinkler sprayed water over her ugly brown yard and over her huge ugly son who lay out in the grass with his big bare feet propped on the end of her chair. Occasionally Mrs. Hopper laughed and shook her head from side to side. Just the two of them lived there. Mrs. Hopper was a divorcée who had once lived in Chicago. Her son's name was Bo and her cat's name was Cat, after one in a movie she'd seen. She wore big round sunglasses and colorful beads and taught biology at the community college. These were the facts Caroline had gathered for Danny on another assignment. Mrs. Hopper looked normal enough but Danny said that at sundown her yellow hair stood straight up and her teeth grew long and mossy green. He said that her husband hadn't really left like the grown-ups said he had; she had eaten him.

Now CAROLINE WAS thinking about *that* in the dark woods on this black moonless night. The picture in her head of Mrs. Hopper's teeth growing made her shaky, and then came the sick wave of school thoughts: the teachers with their paddles, the squat-necked man in charge. She tried to shut out of her head all the stories she had heard by reciting things. She knew "This Old Man" and "When You Wish Upon a Star." She knew the words to "Don't Say Ain't," which used to be Danny's favorite poem before he learned "Beans, Beans."

Don't say ain't,
your mama might faint.
Your daddy might fall in a bucket of paint.
Your brother might die.
Your sister might cry
and your dog might call the FBI.

But she knew the scary things just would not let her
alone. In fact, only yesterday she'd caught herself needing to
cling to her mother's bare legs while she stood in the yard
talking to Mrs. Hopper.

"Go on now, honey," her mother had said. "Let me talk to
Mrs. Hopper for a sec."

"Lord, please let her call me Gail," Mrs. Hopper said, lift-
ing those big sunglasses. Her eyes were crayoned to look
like a cat's. "I was never cut out to be Mrs. Hopper." Her
mother and Mrs. Hopper both laughed. Mrs. Hopper said she
couldn't wait to get a load of those relatives, and Caroline's
mama said that she could.

"I'll tell you about the relatives since you might not remember them so good from last time," Danny had said that
very morning, his spoon poised over a bowl of Cocoa Puffs.
"They all eat like hogs and Aunt Patricia wants to hug and
slobber all over you. Those *girls*," he whispered the word

like it was a swear, "are just stupid, all of them. Uncle Tim is fat. The only boy cousin is Randy, who's okay except last time he brought a girl." Danny knew these things. If he said Mrs. Hopper was friends with the devil and put him up in her basement then it was so. It gave Caroline a shiver to think of all the secrets he told her late at night when their parents were asleep: hunks of hair from dead people found in the cafeteria ravioli, kids' fingers bent backward by the principal until the bones snapped, parents getting arrested and sent to prison when their children talked too much.

Caroline's mother sometimes referred to the relatives as the dog people because they spent their lives going from show to show with these big scary Dobermans. They were always talking about "the circuit" and such. They had wanted to bring along some of the baby dogs but Caroline's mother said they could not.

"I don't blame you at all!" Mrs. Hopper had said, her tanned bare foot swinging back and forth while she sipped a glass of tea. She had a thin silver chain around her ankle. Caroline was hiding under the bushes near where they sat, a cowgirl hat pulled low to disguise herself. "Just who does this sister-in-law of yours think she is?"

"Doris Day." Caroline's mother laughed and sat down. "Doris Day on the darkest night of her life."

"I have never missed my ex-relatives," Mrs. Hopper said. "Divorce is good for something." Then they began talking about their yards. Mrs. Hopper said next she'd like to pave hers and then paint the grass and flowers in place. Caroline's mother said she pictured something different altogether: new place, new town, new weather.

Not an hour after that the station wagon scraped its awful sound, the car horn blasted several short notes, and Caroline's mother rushed past, her perfume sweet and clean in the still summer heat. Her father followed, the screen door slamming shut behind him. Mrs. Hopper was out in her yard just as she had said she would be, to catch a peek, her hair wrapped in a white towel as she sat in a lawn chair letting the sprinkler spray her tanned legs. Danny made a face and shook his head back and forth when Mrs. Hopper lifted her hand in a wave. Caroline was still looking for some sign that she really was a witch but aside from the big purple beads around her neck and the black thumbnail, which she *said* she got when she accidentally hit herself with a hammer, had not come up with anything.

"Fat as ever," Danny said and nudged Caroline when Uncle Tim caught their mother up in a big hug and lifted her right up off the sidewalk. "Posse's coming," Danny said and sniffed the air, pointed to the walk where they all stood. Caroline counted eight of them if you included that bald-headed spit-up-smelling baby.

"I smell 'em all right." Danny swung his legs over the banister. "You keep a watch while I blaze the getaway trail and set up camp." He pointed to the rubber tomahawk strapped to his belt. Then he jumped down behind the box shrubs and was gone, scrambling on hands and knees to the back of the house.

Caroline was on the verge of following when her parents called to her, all the relatives lined up and waiting, baskets of food and a box of diapers at their feet. It was like playing firing squad that time when Danny tied a dish towel over her face and leaned her back against a tree and had all those boys from his neighborhood club lined up and ready for his signal. "When you hear the shots, you gotta fall out and be dead," he had whispered, and then she waited. She waited until the whole yard was silent, bracing herself for the jump. "I'm getting tired," she finally called. "Go on and shoot, okay?" No answer. "Danny!" She had screamed his name until her face felt hot. The yard was silent, and when she finally got free, Danny and the Indian Scouts were nowhere in sight. It was against all the rules to tattle so that night she asked Danny why he had tricked her. He said it wasn't a trick, it was a test. It was the first test, being still and being quiet, and she had passed.

The relatives had gotten out of the car and stood around nodding exactly like those spring-neck dogs that the man who owned the meat market had in the back window of his car. "I ain't having nothing to do with these relatives," Danny had said last night when he crept into her room and knelt by the bed. He said the word "relatives" the same way he spit out "love," so quick it didn't linger in his mouth. "I'm pretending they ain't even here and you better do the same, Caroline." He pronounced her name with two syllables, *Care-line*. She could see by the yellow glow of the night-light as he knelt there how his jaw clenched as he reeled off the rules. "You gotta ask Uncle Tim how much he weighs. Ask Patricia how come she looks and smells so much like her dogs. Don't talk to the girl with the baby at all."

"CAROLINE." HER MOTHER was smiling but Caroline knew from the tone in her voice that she was getting impatient. "And where did Danny run off to?"

Caroline gripped the banister and stepped slowly onto the second step. This was test number two and she knew that Danny was somewhere watching, at the corner of the house or up the pine tree where he kept his secret information. But even worse than that was the fact that Mrs. Hopper was watching, her big slick magazines hiding her bare stomach as she waved.

"What have you done to your shirt?" Caroline's mother smoothed the wrinkled collar. "And where are your shoes? Where is your brother?" Caroline shook her head, shrugged. Danny was watching, and if she messed up, he'd never let her be the maiden scout; she'd have to represent the posse of white men for the rest of her life. Mrs. Hopper had her eyes closed now but that didn't mean anything. She could cast a hex any old time.

"My, my, grown like a weed," Uncle Tim said and shook his head. "You're a cute little boy now aren't you?" They all laughed and Caroline stared at him, reached down to her hip where very soon she'd have her own tomahawk.

"Don't tease her. She's a pretty thing. Got hair like us, Jimmy." Aunt Patricia patted Caroline's father on the arm and then she stepped closer, her arms swooping like a great white hawk as she caught Caroline in a cloud of high-smelling flea powder. Caroline pulled and twisted away before the Great White Hawk could begin to slobber.

"Caroline, can't you say something?" her mother asked and she nodded and again touched the place her weapon would hang at her side.

"You remember Cousin Randy."

The tall one, long legs like a posse rider and hair hanging his shoulders, stepped forward. He wore his hair long and ∙ds around his neck to trick the real Indian Scouts. He round black eyes.

"And this is his girlfriend, Sarah."

Another trick. Her hair was in braids, her feet in leather strapped shoes. She wore Indian jewelry and carried a Frisbee.

"And this is Cousin Sue and little Paul Jr."

Sue looked like the Thin White Hawk and Paul Jr. was a poor excuse of a papoose.

"Come meet little Paul."

"How much do you weigh?" she asked loudly and pointed at Uncle Tim.

"Caroline?" Her mother's arms were around her now and steering her up onto the porch. "I'm sorry, Tim, who knows what gets into them."

"The devil, I guess," her father said and shook his head. He glanced over at Mrs. Hopper when he said that, a sure sign that he knew something about what went on in her basement. She had the straps of her suit undone and they swung forward as she bent to rub lotion on her legs. There was a moment when she was looking right at Caroline, a moment when their eyes locked. *It only takes a minute for her to put the devil in you. It can happen so fast nobody knows until it's too late.*

Now, IN THE black dark, Caroline was crouched down in the pine straw trying not to make a sound. She was looking for the devil, looking for a snipe. She felt something brush against her bare legs, leaves or snipe feathers or snakes or mosquitoes.

"Our mosquitoes are so big," her daddy was famous for saying, "they roll up your pants legs to bite you."

She swatted with her hand and moved her feet away from whatever was down there. She thought of Mrs. Hopper sitting up in a tree, a long black cape blowing around her and wild-eyed cats sitting on the limbs, and her leg jerked.

"Will you stop?" Danny whispered, his voice still deep. "How are we gonna catch a snipe with you making all this noise?"

"You talked," she whispered. "I wasn't talking."

"You were moving. Moved your feet and moved your hand."

She knew the expression on his face as if they were standing in broad daylight, his blue eyes glaring, the sharp bone of his jaw clenched so that the pale purple vein in his cheek could be traced as easily as if it had been put there with a ballpoint pen.

"You let your hand off the bag and messed up the hole. Snipe ain't coming unless it sees a big dark hole."

"Yes sir," Uncle Tim with the fat red face had said. "I myself bagged five big snipe one night. Nobody else ever bagged five." Instead of standing behind their uncle and making faces, Danny had sat on the floor right by his feet, laughing and slapping his leg. Caroline wasn't sure if Danny was pulling a trick or really liking Uncle Tim, and he wouldn't even give her a sign to let her know. He said that he didn't think he ought to have to eat at any children's table with her; he wanted to do what the men were doing.

"What's a snipe anyways?" Caroline asked and waited, her face going warm while they all laughed.

"She don't know nothing," Danny said. "She hasn't even been to school. She doesn't even know what a snipe is." He rolled on his back and laughed his deep laugh. "Tell her, Uncle Tim. Tell her what a snipe is."

"All right." Uncle Tim stared hard at Danny and then looked around the room. "A snipe, Miss Caroline, since you're the only one here that don't know, is a great big brown bird. Well, it's so big you don't even want to call it a bird. It's more like an animal with great big wings."

"Yeah," Danny said and turned to her, nodding with each word, his face flushed and short bangs cowlicked.

Now SHE LONGED for the yellow lamplight of the living room, the warm kitchen where her mother and the other women talked and handed plates back and forth over soapy water that filled the sink. "Jesus Christ," she whispered and ran her hand through her hair just like she had seen Danny do earlier. She waited for him to respond, but he kept his vow of silence and simply pressed down on the toe of her shoe with his foot.

"I said Jesus Christ, oh Jesus Christ, Jesus Christ."

"Call on somebody you know," he whispered harshly, another thing he had learned at school.

"MOON LOOKS RIGHT for sniping tonight," Uncle Tim had said and Caroline went to peek out the window at the thin sliver of a moon just above the trees. It was the fairy-tale moon, or so she'd always heard, never heard of a snipe moon, but there it was, thin, white, and waiting. It sent a chill over her scalp.

"Can't snipe alone," their father said, and Caroline froze, part of her wanting so bad to go; it was the same part of her that wanted to be in the first grade and have a book sack to carry. But then there was that other side, the school dungeon and Mrs. Hopper's nighttime teeth and a big brown animal like a rhinoceros with wings.

"Go with me, Dad," Danny said. "Let's me and you and Uncle Tim and Randy all go."

"Just the men, huh?" the girlfriend asked and came to stand beside Caroline. "Girls can bag a snipe as good as a man. Right?"

Caroline nodded with her, this grown-up girl, so grown that she carried a purse and put stuff on her eyelids. She had unbraided her hair and now it waved like a princess's almost to her waist.

"She's too young to go," Danny said and pointed at Caroline. "Leave her out of it."

"Can't be done," Uncle Tim said and lit a cigar. "You see, you can't hold both sides of the bag when the snipe flies in 'cause he'd knock your socks off. You got to have a person on each side."

"But you gotta have a strong person," Danny said. "Like you."

"Can't be done, son," their father said and went to sit beside Uncle Tim. "You see, once you get to be a certain size, oh I'd say about Randy's height, then you're too big to go sniping because the snipe'll see you there holding the bag. They're smart, those snipe. They aren't gonna come if they think somebody's holding the bag."

"Yes sir, Danny," Uncle Tim locked his hands behind his head and stretched his legs. "Take advantage of the fact that you're just the right age for a snipe hunt. It's one of those things you remember for the rest of your life, like catching a great big fish or hitting a home run." Uncle Tim looked at their daddy and grinned. "A few other things."

"I've done those things," Danny said, his face so serious. "Done both of those, caught a fish at camp and I hit home runs all the time."

"Well then, let's get you out in the woods to bag a snipe."

"But Caroline hasn't. She hasn't caught a fish or hit a home run."

"But I can do it," she had said suddenly, her heart beating faster and faster with the thought of it all.

Now it seemed like she had been in the woods forever. A mosquito bit her on the leg and she let him, without slapping or saying a word. It just wasn't a good night for snipe. Deep down she hoped one didn't come. It was too hot and too dark; the snipe were going to fly into somebody else's bag. Again, something rustled against her leg. She tried to think of something good—the big box of fireworks. She was going to eat a slice of watermelon and sit on the porch rail and watch those fireworks sizzle way up into the sky. She was ready to go.

"They ain't coming," she whispered.

"Not if you keep talking," he said, but this time his voice was slower like he was getting tired of standing in one place, too. "This is the right spot," their father had said. "Don't move from this spot."

"I gotta pee," she whispered, but he ignored her. "Danny? Danny, I really do gotta pee."

"Shhh, one's coming."

She froze in place and sure enough she heard something way down the path, a rustling sound, and she imagined that big animal bird creeping along ready to suddenly fly up and into a hole just like they'd said. She could hear Danny breathing, her own heart beating up in those soft spots of her forehead. She couldn't stand it anymore.

"I can't wait. I gotta go."

"Go in your pants," he said.

"I can't go in my pants. Mama'll get me."

"I'll get you if you don't shut up," he whispered. "I'll tell the principal you been bad, too. I'll tell the witch to come get you. I'll tell you a lot of things you don't want to hear, okay?"

Caroline swallowed hard, blinked back the tears and crouched forward to squeeze her legs together. "I can't wait. I can't hold it."

"Here." He took her side of the bag. "Go over yonder and pull down your pants. Pee out there but be quiet."

"Come with me."

"I can't, you big baby. I gotta hold the bag. How do we know that a snipe ain't been watching this hole the whole time?"

Caroline took a step away and moved her hands through the air to make sure there was nothing there. She eased down the zipper of her shorts.

"I talked to the witch today," she whispered. "She's planning to pour cement all over her yard."

"Yeah right," he said. "Go on now. You're too close. Go away from here so the snipe don't see you."

She took another step and then squatted, feet apart, pants around her knees and held forward. Now she couldn't go. Something was tickling around her legs. She heard another rustling sound from in the woods, closer and closer.

"I talked to her the day you put me in front of the firing

squad, too," she whispered, expecting him to tell her to shut up, but he was listening now. "She was right there in our yard and I never even heard her walk up. She's the one untied me."

His silence scared her and she hurriedly—without going —pulled up and zipped her pants, relieved to take her side of the bag and feel him there beside her.

"She said, 'Oh my poor darling,' not mean at all."

"She ain't a witch," he whispered now. "I lied about all that."

She nodded.

"And I lied about first grade, nothing happens in first grade. Bunch of babies learn to say letters and crap."

"Really?" She turned now and stared at him, angry for the joke but so relieved she wanted to scream and dance.

"But now I know something real that's bad," he said. "I swear to God."

"Tell me," she whispered not really wanting to hear; she was hoping her dad would come running down the path but there was nothing beyond the darkness.

"You gotta cross your heart and hope to die," he said. "If you tell it I'll kill you myself."

"I won't tell."

"Promise? Swear to God?"

That was something else he'd learned at school and their mother had told him not to say it. Now he was waiting for her to say it.

"Swear to God."

"Swear to God," she whispered and waited.

"Mama is about to make us leave." He stared straight ahead. "I heard her tell Mrs. Hopper that as soon as school starts and you ain't scared anymore that she's gonna take us and move across town, maybe even to a new town. But that all depends on how we're doing in school and how Dad is doing all by himself. She told Mrs. Hopper that she had had all she could take. She said she does not love him at all. She said the only good thing he ever did was have us."

Then, before Danny could say more, there was a rustling down on the path, a sudden sound like giant wings rushing forward. It seemed the sound was getting louder, closer, the trees closing in.

"Shit, here it comes," Danny whispered.

Caroline froze to the sounds, unable to move, closer and closer, a rush of big brown wings, a head the size of a bear.

"Snipe!" Danny called, his voice cracking with fear.

It was coming; it was coming, racing up from the woods on its big long legs to jump in the bag, there, over there, out of the woods and right in the path. She straightened too fast and peed in her shorts. A warm stream ran down her leg and into her sneaker but she was too afraid to care. The snipe ducked back into the woods and it was quiet again; Danny was breathing hard.

"I wet my . . ."

"Shhhh!"

There was silence and they waited again. Caroline moved closer to Danny. Now she couldn't even run down the path to their house because the snipe was out there, just there and waiting to catch her and spread his big brown wings and fly away.

"You stink," Danny whispered. "Snipe ain't coming because you stink."

But his voice had lost all anger now, and she knew he was scared, too. "I couldn't help it."

She was about to tell him that he was nothing but a baby, too, when up from the bushes sprang a snipe as big as a man. Caroline jumped toward Danny, getting tangled in the sack and pulling both of them to the ground.

"Daddy!" Caroline screamed as loud as she could, screaming and crying as a dim beam of light moved from side to side on the path and finally stopped on Danny's pale face.

"Can't catch a snipe that way," Uncle Tim said. "No sir, sure can't." And then they were all there, all the relatives laughing and stepping forward. Caroline ran forward and grabbed hold of her mother, momentarily forgetting that her pants were wet.

"I almost had one," Danny screamed. "He was right here, right at the bag, and Caroline had to go and pee in her pants and scare him off."

"I didn't mean to scare it," she said. "Really."

"Come on, now." Caroline's father took her hand and led her down the path. Her mother took her other hand.

"We've still got the fireworks," their mother said and patted Danny's back, pushed him along. "And watermelon and homemade ice cream."

"And snipe," Uncle Tim said. "We got ourselves a big bag of imaginary snipe."

Danny clasped his hands to his ears, his thin face mad and twisted up while he tried not to cry. "Stop! Stop doing this to me."

"It's a joke, son," their father said. "It's just a joke we've been playing in this family for years. Besides, you're one to talk about creeping around and playing tricks."

"You mean there wasn't a snipe out there?" Caroline asked, and then turned to Danny. "What about all the other things?"

"What things, baby?" her mother asked.

"Lord, these clowns have been wanting to pull this trick every summer since Danny was born," Aunt Patricia was telling Cousin Randy's girlfriend.

Uncle Tim reached out to shake hands but Danny turned and ran inside letting the screen door slam shut behind him.

"Oh well, let's start the fireworks," Uncle Tim said. "That'll bring the boy back out. Snipe hunt is supposed to be fun."

"But it wasn't." Caroline followed Danny into the house. She crept up the stairs and then eased open the door to his room. He was kneeling on the floor by his bed, the burlap bag still clenched in his fist. "Danny?" she called.

"Get outta here."

"It was a joke."

"Don't you think I got ears?" He turned toward her and in the thin strip of light from the doorway she could see his eyes and cheeks glistening. "It ain't a damn bit funny. You can go tell them I said that, too. Go tell I said it ain't a damn bit funny or a damn bit fair!"

She waited and then tiptoed close to the window where she could see the first sky rocket soar up and over the pine trees, as high as the stars. He leaned against the windowsill, chin pressed in his hands, and watched the brief flares of light.

"Don't you sit those pee britches on my bed," he said.

"I won't."

She knelt beside him. His breath came in deep sighs as they watched the bright sizzling colors splash in the sky. They could hear their mother calling for them to come outside, but Caroline didn't answer.

"You stink." He shook his head, sighed again.

"I know it," she said and then stayed quiet, relieved that he was talking to her at all.

"That was a dumb joke." He leaned close to the window and stared down at where their parents were standing side by side, their dad's arm looped around their mother's waist. "I can't believe they tricked us like that."

"Danny?" She waited, wondering exactly what she was going to ask him, while her mother stood in the yard and twirled a sparkler round and round. "Is what you told me a trick?"

He stared at his hands, then at the burlap bag for a long time before answering. Now Aunt Patricia and the cousins had sparklers and were writing their names in the sky.

"I told you that you don't have to be a scared baby if I'm there, right?"

She nodded, wanting more from him but that was all he said. She held on to his sticky arm and he didn't even push

her away. So she inched even closer and rested her chin on
the burlap sack, a wash of comfort leaving her drowsy and
looking forward to the feel of clean cotton sheets, the buzzing conversation of the adults downstairs, and the pop and
whine of fireworks that would continue throughout the
night.

Chickens

THE HONEYMOON WAS over before it began. The sweep of bridal frenzy—a wave of white tulle and bone china and petits fours—receded leaving a litter of soggy napkins and a half-eaten cake.

For Lisa the planning had been like a drug, each day upping the dosage, each dose successfully veiling any fears or doubts or anxieties about what she was about to do with the rest of her life. Her energy kicked in full force just as out-of-town relatives arrived; they came in carloads, moved into the Red Carpet Inn and Bell's Econo Lodge. They toasted her, gave her gifts, wished her a long and happy life. She had never before received so much attention and now as she sat in the passenger seat, seeing Alan and the gold ring on his finger that matched her own, she was shocked. She had almost forgotten that he was a part of it all. It was *her* wedding. She planned it; her parents paid for it. She was hungover from too much excitement and too little sleep. The spinning world had slammed to a halt and thrown her for a loop. Her mind had not ventured beyond those moments in the church; she had not looked beyond the stained-glass windows she had studied her entire childhood when the sermons were too boring or too threatening to absorb. Noah, Jonah, Moses, Jesus. They were all there.

But where was she?

They had flown to Pennsylvania (a state she had never in her life visited), rented a car, and now here they were driving through the Poconos. This had been her idea (Alan vetoed her first choice of Niagara Falls) and now she knew she had made a terrible mistake. These mountains were not so great. They were no better than the mountains of western North Carolina or the Shenandoah Valley, where she had visited relatives every autumn when she was a kid. Now, looking at these foreign mountains depressed the hell out of her. Now, with mounting horror, she wondered what in the hell she had done.

"I knew this was a mistake," Alan said, as he slowed down,

and she jerked to attention, afraid he'd read her thoughts. But he was talking about the hotel up ahead, which looked nothing like the pictures at the back of the brides magazines. "Look, there's not even anybody parking cars or carrying luggage." This was no big deal for her. That she might someday wake up and have to stop waiting on herself was a foreign thought. When Alan finally found somebody to get their bags, a slouched teenage boy who wore jeans and a Hard Rock Cafe T-shirt, she had already carried everything over near the big front door. "It was the principle," Alan said. He tipped the boy less than he would have had he been wearing a little monkey suit and cap, and they went over to the lengthy check-in line, joining the crying babies and chain-smoking women in pool attire.

ALAN HAD DONE all of this once before so the wedding preparation had not been something that held his interest. He had surfaced periodically with the voice of experience—make sure the bridesmaid dresses are selected with the least-attractive girl in mind, "nothing worse than one tall lean beauty in chiffon followed by a bunch of pastel stuffed sausages"—and then he would follow up with an anecdote about when he and Susan Hunter Malloy got married. Of course, Susan Hunter knew all of these things because she had older sisters and not only were all of them married but they had all made their debuts in Raleigh.

And where are they now all these decades later? Lisa had wanted to ask. *Sipping tea with the queen?* But that would have been acknowledging that her future husband was also quite a bit older. He was fourteen years older, in fact, which early on had seemed a positive thing. She had actually been surprised that such a smart and successful man had been interested in her at all. He had chosen cosmetic surgery as his specialty (he said for aesthetic reasons) and had gotten in early enough to make a small fortune. He and Susan Hunter had wanted to ensure early retirement, beach house, Ivy League colleges for the kids, nice cars. Now Susan Hunter had a huge chunk of all of that. She spent her summers down at the beach with her children, who were closer to Lisa's age. Rumor had it that Susan Hunter had never in her life looked better.

"I guess she does look good," Alan liked to respond to anyone who commented, most recently his college roommate, who had bumped into her while visiting Figure Eight Island. "I gave her the breasts as an anniversary present years ago. The nose for Christmas one year. Tummy tuck to celebrate when she got her interior design degree. The butt lift was right around the corner," he paused. "But, of course, then I met Lisa." He looked at her when he said this and she laughed and shrugged it off because what she was really thinking about was whether to register silver plate as well as sterling and stainless. Her mother said no; why spend time polishing something unless it's the real thing? His mother said yes; it would be nice for little brunches and afternoon events. *Where? At the old folks' home?* She said Alan had not gotten silver plate the first time, but it was because it was back before the big jump in sterling. Alan and Susan Hunter had gotten tons of sterling.

THEY MET AT the Empowerment Workshop, which Lisa was told used to be called something else, but they got a bad rap for not letting people pee when they needed to. It sounded like a tough-love course for people with money, people like Alan. She was there as one of the several undergraduate students hired to man the doors and hand out Kleenex and point out the bathrooms, serve coffee at the breaks. Alan, handsome in a gray pin-striped suit even though all the other people were dressed down, was one of the first to stand and deliver a tragic story about how he had never felt loved as a child, how that Harry Chapin song "Cat's in the Cradle" (he actually sang a few bars) was completely applicable to him. He was all shook up by the end, crying about how he, in turn, had not always been the best father and that, even though he was now a single parent, he wanted to make a difference.

"He's kind of cute," Emily, the graduate student working with Lisa, had whispered. "I'm going to check him out at the break after he's blown his nose and collected himself."

If not for this statement by a studious, sensible girl Lisa admired, she might never have given Alan a second look. She personally did not like the exhibitionist aspect of the Empowerment Workshop. Besides, at the time all she could think about was Randy, whom she had known her whole life and had always assumed she would marry. She was thinking of Randy and the time she sat on the riverbank reading while he ventured out in a rowboat. Not thirty minutes into his journey, he shot a hole in the boat when a snake dropped down from a tree and startled him. Once she knew he was safely back on shore, that scene never failed to make her laugh, and she relied on it when bored and needing to pass the time. She was thinking of Randy at the break while the graduate student dashed by to whisper that she had found someone else, who though not as handsome as the crying man in the pinstripe, was definitely more her type. Lisa absentmindedly served coffee while she watched the student

talking and laughing with a guy who wore a long gray ponytail and Birkenstocks. He had not yet spoken before the
group, because Lisa certainly would have remembered. He
was wearing enough turquoise to sink a ship.

And there was Alan, dry-eyed and cool looking, extend-
ing his hand for a cup of coffee. He had come back from his
inner child and was telling her about his professional life.
Lisa had actually heard of him. Her mother knew women
who had secretly been to the young genius surgeon. Those
who hadn't yet been talked about going. It was the first time
that Lisa had gone out with someone who all women—
young and old alike—were interested in hearing about. At
first her parents didn't trust him. Her dad said there was
something shifty about him, and Lisa's brother, Mike, just
out of high school said "shifty or *shitty?*" Mike was completely devoted to Randy; at times it seemed he was the one
who was enduring a breakup.

"Why are you going out with him?" her mother asked. "It
isn't the money is it?"

"No way," Lisa said.

"Well, why do you guess he's going out with you?"

"What do you mean by that?" She asked. "I'm not good
enough?"

Lisa knew her mother meant well, that what she really

wanted to ask about was Randy and if Lisa had seen him. Her mother had already asked one time too many, sending Lisa into a rage the likes of which she had never experienced in all of her life. "Screw Randy," she screamed, her parents sitting there in the his-and-her recliners they'd given each other for their twenty-fifth anniversary, "everybody else has." Now, her mother knew not to utter a peep.

The truth was that, after years of loyalty, Randy had screwed up and she had caught him. He was going out with other people, had been for over six months. *Randy* Randy, her roommate said. So what if her parents loved him like a son? So what if he had been the one to straighten Mike out back in ninth grade when he was on the verge of trouble?

He said he was unsure of the future. Well, who isn't, she asked. He said he had *accidentally* slept with a girl who lived right there in Lisa's dorm. She had yet to figure that one out. Over and over he kept asking what he was going to do. Take over his dad's land and farm? Go to vet school? Or should he just chuck all of that and take some time off, maybe trek cross-country, camp some, visit a few friends? Regardless of what he chose—if history counted for anything—he'd change his mind in a month or two.

The hardest part of the breakup was that she and Randy had all of the same memories and points of reference, and though she tried to cut him away from her thoughts like tearing a face from a photo, it was impossible. Everything she knew about boys and what they liked or didn't like came straight from Randy. If people saw her, they asked about him, and vice versa. She had been the one part of his life that he remained faithful to, or so she had always thought. Now she was beginning to wonder.

BUT RANDY WAS trying to find himself, a euphemism Lisa despised. That's what everybody on the soap operas was doing—trying to find themselves. Whenever a character said that, all the girls clustered in the dorm TV room sent up a scream of deafening cackles. She made the mistake of telling all of her friends about Randy, not knowing that many of them already knew. Many of them, in fact, were secretly hoping to hear from him themselves. They called him a hunk; they called him a fox. It was a mistake to have aired her laundry because late that spring when he came back around, still unsure about what to do with his life but certain that he wanted to get back together, her pride got in the way of what she really wanted to do. "Well, think about it," he said. "I'll be around." The girls on her hall called him a rounder. They called him a chick magnet.

At the time she convinced herself that she was acting on

her own desires, only to later worry that she had let her fears about what the other girls would think (girls she'd probably never see again in her life) overpower her own feelings. She put him off a few more times, thinking the suffering would make him want her even more and would definitely teach him not to ever do that to her again. She did not return his call even though more than anything she missed their late nights at *The Rocky Horror Picture Show,* where they dressed up and acted out all the parts like the hundreds of other cult followers crammed into the small dark theater on Main Street on campus. After the show, they used to go to Snoopy's, a popular hangout that stayed open all night long. Sometimes they sat there until the sun came up. Sometimes they talked about what their future would be like—the house (a cabin built right near the river, the back porch facing westward so that they would watch the sun go down over the tobacco fields that he would one day own), the brood of kids (at least five), the dogs (the bigger the better). The Rocky Horror party they would throw every Halloween. Sometimes they talked about things that had happened back in grade school or junior high, stories and gossip about people in their hometown, using their own shorthand that was guaranteed to shut out anyone else around. She had never even thought what life would be like without those stories.

And then she heard that Randy had been dating all along, that he had been seeing the same girl for several dates, a Chi O from Richmond, a tiny, tanned Chi O with a 3.7 grade point average who drove a little red Karmann Ghia and was madly in love with Randy. Why did people feel the need to tell her all of this? Was it like that story her father used to tell about chickens in the barnyard, how they can all be living in harmony and then if one starts bleeding they all rush in and peck it to death? He told that, of course, to make Lisa and Mike sensitive to the weaknesses of others. It translated to *Don't bully or tease people; be someone who steps in and defends what's right.* But she had never imagined that she would one day be the bleeder, that she would spend three days cooped in her room without taking a shower or changing her clothes. Her suitemate, a girl known for her impeccable taste and fastidious hygiene and clearly well versed in the rules to being a good person, insisted that she get up and wash her hair and get dressed. And the next week, with Lisa still not out of the woods, that same girl insisted that she take the job as door watcher for the Empowerment Workshop. The only other choice for campus volunteers was door watcher for the evangelist who was coming right before summer. JERRY IS COMING SOON, the signs read. Jerry, she later heard, claimed to have received a letter from God that was written on the back of a Twix candy wrapper. *Spread the word, Jerry,* the letter said.

How different her life would have been if she had gone to that one. There certainly wouldn't have been a date to come out of it. Instead she would have called Randy to see if he remembered the time a boy in their school pretended to be blind so that he could then be healed and attempt to heal others, right during the basketball game halftime. Randy would have remembered the boy's name and who they had been playing and then they would have pretended that nothing had ever happened. He would have come over to get her and they would have gone to get a pizza and that would have been that.

When she met Alan, he talked a lot about the real world and about how so many kids her age had no idea what they were in for when they were actually expected to work and participate in adult venues. "Except someone like you, of course," he added. He made her feel smart and mature. He constantly commented on her appearance, saying how she was someone he wouldn't dream of raising a scalpel to; there was nothing to perfect. She didn't believe that, but still it was enough to make her want to keep her brows plucked and her legs waxed, to primp and preen as she had watched her suitemate do. She never mentioned Randy to Alan, except to say that she had known him her whole life and that the relationship had ended because he had needed some time to find himself.

"Oh please," Alan said, "I haven't said that since I was fifteen." At the time she was still so hurt and angry at Randy that she relished hearing someone else attack him. Randy could not afford one of Alan's shoes, not to mention the pearl and diamond earrings he gave her. Randy's idea of a good present had been water skis and a thong bikini she had never had the nerve to wear. She was impressed by Alan's good looks and his Italian suits (though she never would have known their nationality if not told), the gray Volvo he insisted she drive because it was so much safer than her Dodge Dart, the places he took her for dinner (her suitemates begged her to order big and then get doggie bags).

Still, she had those moments when she felt washed in homesickness and desperate to reclaim what had always been hers. She wished herself back to her hometown, where she and Randy used to get food from Taco Bell and then sit out in the middle of Hollydale Cemetery, where they leaned against the side of the only mausoleum in the place. They had been going there since the fifth grade when they chalked their initials in the cool marble slab and vowed that every word spoken in this place was top secret. It was their place, something they had never told another living soul about. But by graduation she had put Randy out of her mind and instead was trying to decide what to do with her life. Teach high school French as her diploma entitled her to do? Go to graduate school?

She had gotten used to riding along beside Alan. She was used to the way the soft leather of the seats felt against the backs of her legs, the way the car smelled clean and like the cologne Alan wore (Aramis) and not like stale beer and cigarettes and wet dog. He talked at great length about his work and about his clients (swearing her to secrecy) and about his ex-wife, who was trying to bleed him dry. It made her feel more mature than she had ever imagined being. She felt secure in the knowledge from one day to the next that someone was planning where she would eat and what she would do, and sometimes even what she would wear. She had read that many women seek this, a comfort zone that enables them to exist without physical hardships or worries. Then they can focus on the part of themselves that is creative and independent; they can raise children in a comfortable nest.

She was living at her parents' after graduating so she was still privy to all the hometown news: Randy had brought a girl to meet his family. They went with his mother to church on Sunday even though Randy hadn't been to church in years. Lisa knew from the descriptions that it was the same Chi O girl and she confirmed it herself when she rode by his parents' house late that Sunday night when she couldn't sleep and saw the little red car parked there. She stopped at the corner and waited, half hoping that Randy would see her sitting there.

Later that same week, she heard that Randy was applying to veterinary school and was going to take a year off in the interim. Work a little, move in with the girlfriend, who would be starting graduate work in the fall. She saw him at the A & P soon after hearing this and crept up behind him, placed her hands over his eyes, but before he could even guess, the girlfriend was standing beside him, her arm looped through his. "You must be Lisa," she said without really cracking a smile. "Randy has told me all about you, all about your little secret places like the one we went to today —creepy— and your secret languages from grade school. Cute." If his eyes showed any apology for his betrayal she didn't see it, and after a polite exchange—he asked her if she was still involved with the "plastic doc"—she dashed out of the store, abandoning her cart behind the greeting-card stand.

So of course she said yes when Alan asked her to move in with him. Who wouldn't? After all, here was this successful, nice-looking person ready to take care of her for life. And marriage made the most sense of all. What she had with Randy was a kid thing; intellectually she knew that this was the choice that made the most sense for her. So she read *Bride* magazine cover to cover, and the thought of herself in one of those dresses, the wonderful place settings to choose from, the whole prospect of buying her very own house with window treatments and furniture thrilled her beyond belief and took up a good chunk of her time. She would have to think about school or a job later, *after* the wedding. She might even decide not to get a job at all, ever, a luxury she had never dreamed of having.

Randy sent her a wedding gift—a doormat that said "Wipe Your Paws" and a cookbook with all of Elvis Presley's favorite meals called *Fit for a King*. She had not shown Alan these, fearing what he might say, though for several late nights, she scoured the pages of the cookbook for a hidden message—anything, a hair from his head, a turned down page that might lead her to read every word for the message. She told herself that if there was not a sign, she should let go and move on.

"Are you sure this is what you want?" her mother had asked, and though she had a chilling moment when she wanted to voice her uncertainty, she had a sudden image of Randy bumping along the fields in his truck with the Chi O, showing her all of the places and telling her all of the things they had sworn to keep secret, and it made her sink her heels deeper. It made her turn her attention to some more expensive choices: she went from Gorham to Wedgwood. Everyone got cold feet. She studied all the travel ads in the back of the magazines. Alan had said that they could go anywhere on their honeymoon—anywhere she wanted to go.

"Niagara Falls or the Poconos." She had stated her choices firmly so that he wouldn't talk her into some place like Italy or Hawaii, places she might want to visit as an older person. And of course going to a place known for honeymoons was corny but that was part of the fun of it all. She imagined they would take photos of the two of them lounging in a heart-shaped tub. It would be the sort of thing you could pull out and laugh about for the rest of your life. Alan said he had taken Susan Hunter on a cruise, and even though he could not afford it at the time, the two of them had always been so happy that they splurged and did it up big.

"Well, this is what I want," she said and showed him all the pictures in the magazines. "There is a swimming pool right in your room."

"Oh God," he sighed his worldly sigh and laughed. "If this is what you want then, okay."

There was condescension in his voice; she heard it loud and clear, but she would prove him wrong. Now, as she stood looking around the hotel entryway, she anticipated his saying *I told you so*. It looked nothing like the pictures. It looked as much like the Bates Motel as it did the pictures. She had read recently that Janet Leigh never showered after making *Psycho*. Who could blame her? Janet was in *Psycho* and Tony Curtis played the Boston Strangler. No wonder Jamie Lee Curtis wound up making those Halloween movies. She said all of this to Alan, but he claimed to know nothing about cult movies and horror shows. He only knew *films* and he was likely to *not* like what other people liked. He called it discriminating. There was a time less than a year ago when she would have called it boring. Randy would have said *So who died and made you the goddamn authority?*

Heart-shaped tubs and round beds. Fireplaces. Jacuzzis. It was clear that at one time this place had been *the* place to go—like maybe in the sixties. The nightclub entry was lined with photos of stars who had visited in the past: Milton Berle, Soupy Sales, and Charo, one of the most recent, the giggling Spanish woman who got famous by screaming "kichie kichie" while beating on a guitar and wearing next to nothing.

While they waited, Alan commented that Lisa looked sad

and then explained that what she was feeling was a kind of postpartum after all the excitement of the wedding. He said that Susan Hunter had experienced something very similar after their wedding and after the births of both children. "It's one of those female things," he said. Randy would have had something sarcastic to say back to that, something smart and cynical. She realized then that part of her honeymoon fantasy had always been that Randy would *be* there. Other than family vacations, she had never traveled anywhere *without* him. He loved nothing better than a road trip.

Once during her sophomore year in college, they had headed out with no destination in mind. At every fork, he'd ask her to choose *left* or *right*. They finally wound up near the beach on old Highway 301 in what looked like a ghost town of little pastel cinder-block buildings. Other than the Days Inn where they got a room, there was a rundown shopping center with a grocery store and Laundromat. When they asked the person at the motel desk what there was to do, she pointed them in the direction of what she called the arcade. It was an old gas station that now housed several pinball machines and a pool table. The main attraction was the dancing chicken. Deposit a quarter outside its glass cage and kernels of corn were made available behind a chute that would open if the chicken danced over the red button on the floor. Sometimes the chicken kept dancing even when the chute was empty. It reminded Lisa of the story of the red shoes and that poor girl who couldn't stop dancing; her choices were to dance herself to death or to cut off her feet. They had so much fun that they came back the next semester with several friends in tow. Nothing had changed. Not even the sheets on the motel beds, they joked. But that was before they went to the arcade to find that the dancing chicken had been replaced by a big rat snake who occasionally ate a live mouse but otherwise did nothing. There was a sign saying DON'T TAP THE GLASS so of course everyone did. They never saw anyone who actually worked at the arcade, so there was no way to find out what happened to the chicken. Lisa was sure that it had danced itself to death. Randy suggested that it had eaten itself to death, that maybe a tour bus of lost but well-meaning travelers pumped quarter after quarter into the slot. Or maybe somebody got hungry one night and wrung its neck, fried it up. Either way, it was gone.

FINALLY THEY WERE all checked in just in time for a flock of kids to rush past and into a room off of the lobby as big as a skating rink and just as loud. There was a clown entertaining children. He had a cotton-candy machine. There was a popcorn machine. There were canisters of helium for balloons that he twisted and shaped into animals that children wore on their heads. There was a magician and someone who could cornrow the girls' hair and apply henna tattoos. It was a bar mitzvah. Oy. Funny what manhood looks like from a distance.

This was so *not* what she had expected but she clung to the notion of the little pool in the room and how she was going to stretch out on that round bed fully clothed and fall into a deep deep sleep. She didn't care if she slept through the honeymoon night and on into the next day. All she wanted now was sleep and rest. It was the postwedding jitters, that was all, and come morning, she would be okay again. She would see, by the light of day, that she had made the right decision, that this was the beginning of a wonderful life together.

But they had only an hour left to be served in the dining room, so Alan checked their bags and off they went down mazes of hallways, following signs for the restaurant. Outside the door to the restaurant, where they had to wait in line yet again, there was someone drawing caricatures, someone selling costume jewelry, and a psychic. Her little sign said ASK ROSE and there were other little signs featuring comments from satisfied customers. Things like ROSE SAVED MY LIFE,

POCONOS ROSE KNOWS, I WILL NEVER SAY NEVER AGAIN. Apparently Rose did palms, tarot, or she would simply talk to you about what lay ahead.

Lisa was watching several women huddled together waiting their turn. Rose looked up and directly at her. The gaze was so strong and intentional, Lisa looked around to see if there might be someone else Rose was staring at. There was no one else. Alan had struck up a conversation with the couple in front of them, a couple closer to his age who were also disappointed in the accommodations. Lisa attempted a smile to acknowledge the dark gaze but Rose just lifted her chin as if to say *I know your secret.*

Lisa was leaning toward the ASK ROSE table, but then Alan was pulling her into the dining room and over to a far, darkened corner he had tipped the maître d' to get. "What is it?" he asked, but she didn't dare tell him what she was thinking. That she felt her mind had been read. That perhaps this woman knew more than she did, or maybe knew what Lisa wasn't willing to admit to herself. She just said that she was tired. And when they were finally served and finished and about to head up to the bridal suite, all of the vendors in the hallway were gone, leaving little cardboard placards with their hours and specialties behind. She stood staring at the sign for Poconos Rose, hoping for some clue, some reason to believe she was a total phony and that the look she gave Lisa meant absolutely nothing.

Their room was drab with stained wall-to-wall carpeting, old floral spread and drapes (red and yellow). It was something not so different from what you'd see in a Days Inn. Back then, with Randy, it was funny. Back then she didn't feel embarrassed the way she did now as she and Alan stood in the doorway. He wanted to lift her over the threshold but she reminded him of his bad back. Anyway, she was very busy taking in the disappointing sights. There was a cheap painting of a mountain scene. There was a bidet but this was not a bidet of elegance; rather, it was more like a kind of sex-hygiene thing—quick spritz and you're ready for more. She could die. She sat on the bed and started crying and when she did Alan was right there behind her, telling her how he understood. He didn't even say *I told you so*.

He said, "Don't worry. Honeymoons can be a bit of a let-down."

She excused herself, locked the bathroom door, and looked around in disgust. Where were the heated tile floors they had advertised? The towel warmers? The European spa towels? Where was the round bed with gossamer netting to make you feel you were floating on a cloud? Was she the first person to ever feel this way? This washover of sick regret?

She dried her eyes and stepped back into the room. She willed herself to picture Randy on this sad evening. He was sitting out on the stoop of his parents' house where the two of them had sat hundreds of nights waiting for steaks to grill and staring out at the pastures and tobacco fields. Poor brooding Randy, heartbroken. He was sorry now that he had not stepped forward and intervened. He would always regret it; one day he would tell her so and then she would say that she regretted it, too, and then they would go back to where they had always been—a couple—partners for life. They would not be able to remember which came first, his infidelity or her desire for something more in a relationship. It wouldn't even be important.

She was about to laugh just thinking of the two of them getting back together, but then realized how false that fantasy was—false and hopeless. He probably never even thought of her that day, or if he did it was to decide not to put on a suit and go to the wedding. It probably never crossed his mind that he should go and object, that she might need his intervention.

SHE SHOULDN'T HAVE, but as she lay down beside Alan, she let herself think of being with Randy as they bounced through the fields in his truck, one of his dogs squeezed between them on the front seat. His hair was wild and windblown, and the Marshall Tucker Band blasted from the speakers. They drove down the dirt roads to the river and then sneaked into the old deserted ice plant, a place they believed none of the other kids had discovered, or if they had, hadn't dared to ease through the chained doorway into the cool darkness.

IN THE MORNING, when Alan suggested they go to the exercise room and then sit in the whirlpool awhile, she begged off with extreme, perhaps irrational, fears of community mold and bacteria that incubate in such an environment. She said she would lounge a bit, walk around, but she knew exactly where she was going. Rose had not arrived yet and there was already a line, two of the women who had been there the night before. Lisa felt uncomfortable sitting there eavesdropping so she wandered down the hall and into the ladies' room, where she found Poconos Rose herself, stripped of all makeup and jewelry, brushing her dark hair and twisting it up on top of her head. She was pinning it in place when her gaze in the mirror caught Lisa's.

"Do I know you?" she asked.

"Wouldn't you know that answer?" Lisa answered. When there was no laughter she apologized and started again. "I saw you last night at your table."

"Yeah, it's busy around here," she said. "But the line moves pretty quick if that's what you're worried about."

"No, I'm not worried."

"What then?" Rose pulled a big purse onto the counter and took out her makeup bag. She applied black eyeliner and a maroon-colored lipstick, both items that made her look much older. "I'm priced reasonably."

"Oh no, that's not it," Lisa said. "You were looking at me last night."

"I was?" She put her hand to her chest and squinted as if trying to remember. Her eyes were a brilliant emerald green, clearly contacts.

"Yes, I was in line to go to dinner and I noticed that you were watching me, staring really. I think you saw something."

"Oh?" Rose crossed her arms over her thin chest and studied Lisa from head to toe. "Were you with a guy in a suit? A little older? Kind of executive looking?"

"Yes."

"Newlywed."

"Yes!" Lisa was getting excited.

"That's no vision, honey," she said. "Here's what comes here: you got the newlyweds; you got the old ones trying to recapture the first honeymoon—they're my favorites actually, no offense; you got the bar mitzvah crowd, like last night? Lord. You got an occasional reunion."

"So there wasn't something about me?"

"Should I have seen something?"

"I don't know. I really thought you did." Lisa turned and perched on the edge of an old vinyl chair near the door.

"Sounds like you wanted me to see something."

"Maybe."

"Like maybe you made a mistake?"

Lisa looked up, eyes wide. Rose was not much older than Lisa if at all, but the way she talked, the way she looked Lisa dead in the eye made it clear she had already seen far more than Lisa probably would in a lifetime. She had a hard, muscular stance that made Lisa feel inadequate.

"You think I did?"

"Do you?" Rose threw her lipstick back into her floppy macramé bag, then turned, exasperated by all the questions. "Look. I really have had a vision or two, okay? Else I wouldn't be in this particular business. But what I see in you is what anybody who took two seconds to look could see."

Lisa paused, afraid to ask another question and afraid not

to. "Can you tell me what you see?" She stared down at her hands to avoid Rose's eyes.

"Well okay, last night what I saw was a young woman wearing the kind of suit worn by business women, church ladies, and girls who take the time to plan a going-away outfit. Am I right?" Lisa nodded. "You're clearly not one of the first two, and your husband," she paused, giving the word extra weight, "still had one of those flower things stuck up near his neck."

"Oh. A boutonniere."

"Whatever. You're standing there with your arms crossed over your chest looking like you're at a funeral and concentrating on *my* business instead of your own." She laughed. "And what was I thinking? I was thinking about how I was in a hurry to get to my kid's piano lesson."

"I'm sorry."

"Don't be." She shook her head and smiled. "We've all been there. Maybe this lifetime, maybe another, but we've been there." Rose pulled a multicolored scarf from the bag and draped it over one shoulder. She saw Lisa watching and stopped short again; she seemed to be getting impatient. "Okay, so I dress up a little. Most of those people out there wouldn't pay me the time of day if I didn't look like what they expect me to look like, you know? I mean I'm really a blonde, a natural blonde, but who knows a blond fortune teller?" She leaned close and pointed to her eyebrows, the fair hairs clearly crayoned over with black pencil. "Men are that way. Friends. Mothers. There's a certain look we expect, you know? Sometimes the image is true and sometimes it isn't." She turned her head from side to side, admiring the swirl of her earrings in the mirror. "We're all hoping that we can see beyond what the eye sees, but for most it's just trial and error. You know, you reach a certain age and it's time to fly the coop, no time to think about anything other than that very moment. There's never the perfect time. We'd all do something a little different if given another chance."

"I was fine before the wedding and now all of a sudden I'm terrified. It's crazy."

"Doesn't sound crazy to me." Rose put her bag on her shoulder and took one last look at her reflection. "I'd call it everyday business for somebody like me." She closed her eyes and took several deep breaths, raised her arms up high, and swayed back and forth. "There, I'm ready." She was about to open the door but then turned back once more. "You know, nobody knows everything. If we did there would be no reason to live. At least you weren't too chicken to try. A lot of people are, you know, and what do they wind up with? And remember—you're nothing but a human *bean*—that's what my kid would say. Human *bean*." Rose laughed and disappeared in a swirl of gold and imitation silk. The door wheezed shut, and immediately Lisa could hear the clamoring—a shrill peep of needy people, like chickens at feeding time, pushing to be first in line. Though tempted to turn and look, Lisa shielded her eyes and ran back to the honeymoon suite. If she could just concentrate on what lay immediately before her, she would be all right. If she could just take it day by day, picking and choosing what best suited her life. She wasn't a chicken, and she wasn't about to be pecked to death. And if she felt frightened, Alan would be there with an outstretched palm and a promise that he might, or might not, be able to keep.

Hominids

"I'M THINKING I will have myself a restaurant known as Peckers, and as my model I will use Hooters, where one of Bill's buddies likes to go on Friday night. I will have a woodpecker instead of an owl and waiters instead of waitresses. They will wear uniforms that are, shall I say, a bit revealing below the belt and as manager my job will be saying who looks good in the outfit and who doesn't. Sorry, that's business. It's not harassment if you say right up front that Peckers is all about peckers. The Pecker Burger, the Pecker Shake, the foot-long Peckerdog, the Pecker who serves you. There will be lots of cute puns about wood, redheaded, etc. I think it will be a huge success."

I make this speech to the group—Bill's old friends and

their wives—gathered for the golf weekend Bill pulls together every year. Golf is the excuse for the get-together
even though sometimes only a couple of them actually play.
Most of the time is spent drinking and telling tales. Bill has
just told how he and the boys could not help but pull off of
I-95 and check out Cafe Risqué, which advertises all up and
down the highway. I also say, "So why not South of the Border? They have lots of billboards on the highway, too, and
they have liquor by the drink. They even have fireworks you
can buy. Sombreros. Enchiladas. As a matter of fact, you can
buy just about anything at South of the Border, except for
the señoritas, *unless*," I add, feigning great surprise, "that's
why you went to Cafe Risqué instead."

THE SIGNS SAY that Cafe Risqué is open all night
and that the women are topless. The women on the signs
look like supermodels—shiny healthy hair and white well-
cared-for teeth. I'm certain that what's on the billboards is
not what you find inside, especially at eight o'clock in the
morning, or two o'clock in the afternoon. Or any time, for
that matter. I'm betting you find track marks, illiteracy, scars
of at least one abusive relationship. At least that would be
my uneducated guess.

I'm guessing stretched-out titties, the children who stretched them cold and alone at home waiting for mama to get off work. Or maybe the women have no children and they eye every man who comes in through that darkened glass door as a potential future, a ticket to a better, cleaner existence. Men, for instance, like my spouse, Bill, who is college educated and should know better, and his sidekick, Ed, an old fraternity brother who has flown in from Atlanta and who chooses to spend part of his day this way while his wife and newborn are back at home.

I voice my sadness at this scene. I politely question Bill's participation in this event and ask how he will explain such a place, should the question ever arise, to our son and daughter, who are on the threshold of adolescence. And still the conversation in the room turns to breasts. Ethan—former college fraternity brother from Winston-Salem—just can't get over the whole scene. He is imitating, swinging his pathetic khaki-clad body side to side. He discusses ta-ta size like you might a pumpkin, while his wife stands there and giggles. I catch her eye and she stops cold. She knows better but like many of us she has learned that it's easier to look the other way, pretend that you really did not see or hear what you thought you did.

You can learn a lot on a weekend like this. I look around the room—my dining room—as they gather here for cocktails and hors d'oeuvres, and I might as well be on another planet even though it's a scene I have lived through for over a decade by now.

There is always at least one man going through the motions of separation or divorce. That one normally arrives with a woman twenty years younger or comes alone and flirts with all the wives. This year it is Dennis, from D.C., who grew up in this very town but has gone to great lengths to rid himself of any traces of his native origin. It is as if he has no memory of a mother or a childhood or an education here. He would have the world believe that he simply sprang forth in a business suit with a fat wallet boasting membership in the NRA, a Rolex on his wrist, and a BMW parked by the curb. Right now he seems to be checking out everyone's cleavage. I watch him and keep thinking that before the night is over, I will go and get my high school yearbook and pass it around so everyone can check out when he was a Future Farmer of America and a Teen Dem and a relatively decent guy. I will ask how his mother—a woman who put in forty years as a receptionist at the courthouse and who raised a child all by herself—is faring out at Turtle Bay Nursing Home, which he visits only at Christmas if then. He keeps trying to catch my eye and wink like the two of us are some-how in on something. My glance back at him says *You suck*.

I TELL EVERYBODY that I think men who are at-tracted to breasts in a major way are still yearning to suckle their mamas. Isn't it true there's a whole generation of formula-fed men who never had that opportunity and now they are suffering? They want to latch on; they want to make their mothers draw sharp breaths in with the tight wrench just before that glorious letdown. I say that knowing that they are all Enfamil men with mamas who claim they couldn't nurse when the truth is nobody taught them how. I don't think evolution would have allowed a whole genera-tion to die out; it certainly hasn't happened that way in the animal kingdom. You don't see animals making fun of teats and udders. I doubt if it happens among humans in Third World countries either. But maybe this was the period in his-tory when society began to look at the breast in a whole dif-ferent way. Maybe this is when the breast went from a source of nourishment for the young to something for men to pinch and make jokes about.

I can tell that they are tiring of my lecture; I can feel the tension rising so I choose to sink back and away. I ask them to tell us all about their games that day, no one even noticing that this is a way of defusing the situation, a way for me to sit and sip my drink and fade off into my own thoughts. Like the time I accompanied my son and his third-grade class to the science museum where we stood before the model of Lucy—our first woman—her thumb visible, her body emerging from a previous simian form. She was only three and a half feet tall, her head the size of a softball. She was only in her twenties when she died and already her backbone was deformed; she suffered a terrible form of arthritis. She was found at the edge of a lake and scientists are unsure if she drowned or if she simply died of an illness. Did anyone even consider the possibility that perhaps she grew so tired, her heart so heavy, that she simply lay facedown on the shore and waited for the water to carry her into an eternal sleep? Did such a desire even exist in this early human form or was it the result of years of domestication, demands that went far beyond what life out in the wild would have required? Lucy's breasts were not huge; they were thin and stretched. The kids pointed at her nipples and butt crack. They were children and had that right. They still had every opportunity to grow up and imagine the infant kept alive by Lucy's milk—a whole world's population nourished by Lucy's milk.

• • •

THE DISCUSSION OF golf comes around to the old story about Johnny Carson asking Arnold Palmer what he did for good luck before a match. Palmer replied, "My wife kisses my balls," to which Carson said, "Bet that makes your putter stand up." No one in the room actually saw the interview so we're not sure how much if any of it is true. The discussion of Ethan's swing leads right back into the swing of the hips of the woman who was clearly attracted to him at Cafe Risqué. Then the swing of her breasts, which Ethan said made him think of Loni Anderson. "Not the face, of course," he said. "Jesus Christ."

"Can you give it a rest?" Ethan's wife finally says. She is on her third cosmopolitan and feeling strong if only momentarily.

"So men like breasts," Dennis says and looks around to get moral support. "Is that news? What's the big deal?"

I say that if there were a disease the cure of which required men to have their penises removed they would be a bit more sensitive to body parts. I say this knowing that Dennis's mother had a double mastectomy when he was still in high school; there she was, a divorced mother, not so common at the time, working a forty-hour week, with a disease no one ever mentioned. There were no support groups, no magazine articles in which other women told their stories.

Ethan, who is lounging back on my sofa with his shiny little loafers propped on one silk-upholstered arm and who has had one too many, tells us, apropos of nothing, that he takes Viagra. There is absolute silence. Ethan's wife, Joyce, who had gone to the bathroom (she said, though I know that really she slipped by the liquor cabinet to freshen her drink), now returns to silence.

"What's up?" she asks.

"Ethan apparently," I say, and after the roar of laughter dies down, I continue. "He was just telling us about how he takes Viagra."

"Ethan!" There is horror all over her face. I am horrified just to imagine the man tuned up like an Eveready. Horrified that poor Joyce has to live with him. And now horrified at myself for making a joke at her expense as well as his.

"Do you see blue?" one man asks. "I've heard it can affect your vision."

"Temporary," Ethan answers smugly. Mr. All Knowing. Mr. Thinks He's Big. Nothing can slow him down.

"And it works?"

"Oh, *yeah*, it works." Ethan is enjoying his five minutes in the sun as he and Joyce knock back the liquor for very different reasons.

"So this was for a medical reason?" I ask.

"You mean impotence?" Dennis yells.

"No," Ethan spits. He wants to call me something really really bad, but he thinks better with Bill there beside me. He can't call Dennis anything because Dennis is a rung or two higher than he is on the man's man ladder. "I was just curious."

"Oh," I say. "Curious."

Bill catches my eye and I can't tell if it's to apologize or to say *Give me a break, I only entertain these guys once a year, let us act like boys. Let us have some fun*. I've heard it all before. And there were the years when the women thought the way we could compete was to act just like them, to go to clubs and drink too much and watch men strip. Scream out things like *Wooo wooo woo, shake it baby yeah*, whistle wolf calls, salivate like Pavlovian dogs. You know, you never really do get into that and you sure get tired of trying to. Personally I'd rather be watching old movies—Bette Davis, Charles Boyer. I'd rather be in my nightgown with a mug of hot chocolate and my children snuggled under a down comforter watching reruns of *Andy Griffith* or *Leave It to Beaver*. I can't imagine Andy Taylor or Ward Cleaver going to Cafe Risqué. The long and short of it (no pun intended) is that very often at the end of a day, I am tired. My breasts are tired. My legs, back, brain. I would like nothing better than to stretch out and close my eyes, disappear, if only briefly.

THE MEN, IN spite of everything that has been said, return to the Cafe Risqué topic. Apparently there was one sexy waitress who was considerably overweight. (Ethan: "See? We aren't prejudiced against fat ones. The one that really liked me was the *fat* one.") Another skinny Asian one, Dennis informs us, needs a good orthodontist. (Plus her G-string was nasty looking; her thighs had purple stretch marks.) The one pouring coffee had a tattoo of a snake wrapping around her throat. A really fat ass. I am about to comment about how they all must have left nose prints on the glass of her cage when I walk over and stand next to Bill just in time to hear Ethan deliver his punch line about how to screw a fat girl: "Roll her in flour and look for the wet spots."

"What a hoot!" I slap him on the back as hard as I can. "Aren't you *funny?*" I avoid looking at Joyce, who I have known for a very long time. She was in my wedding. Bill is the godfather of their son. She drinks a little bit more, I notice, at each gathering.

"I've got one for you," I say. "Where do men go after they go to Hooter's?"

"Where?"

"The Hootel. And why don't women date Wood*peckers?*" I emphasize the last two syllables.

"Why?"

"Always boring." The women like that one. "And why does a dog lick his balls?"

"Wait, I know this one," Ron says. "Because he can."

"And did you hear about what happened when the woman showed her size 36C breasts? No? None of you guys have heard this one?"

They all shake their heads, Bill included, as they wait for the punch.

"God, this is an old one. I hear it at least once a week. And I can follow it with the one about the 36B and the 32A and the 48DD."

"So tell us already," Dennis says. He and Ethan are standing there nudging each other like prepubescent boys.

"Well, they all had cancer. They all had to have their breasts surgically removed." The women look down at my rug, the lovely intricate pattern of color. I'm sure there's at least one bad Pap smear in this room. One lump that has caused fear and worry. "Like your mother, Dennis."

They are all quiet now. The women are moving toward the warm yellow glow of my kitchen, where I have promised them a comfortable seat and a glass of good wine while I finish preparing the meal. "Maybe this is the reason the women go to the kitchen," Ron's wife, a relatively new wife, says quietly. "I wish we had done it sooner."

Now you can hear a pin drop. Now you can hear the cars passing on the highway, a rise and fall like ocean waves, and my mind is there by the highway with those women walking around inside Cafe Risqué. And wouldn't any one of them give everything she owned to be standing in this very room, in this privileged life where people actually have hobbies and children fuss about the full plate of good food you put before them and men take for granted the women they married, the bodies they like to roll on top of in the middle of the night, the breasts they pinch and knead like dough.

"Honey," Bill says and calls me back to the doorway. "Let it drop, okay? This is a party, not some New Age awareness group."

Tears spring to my eyes and I have to look away. I look out the window into our backyard at the array of Little Tikes apparatus that no longer gets used. He looks over at all of his buddies, especially Dennis, and laughs as if to apologize for the interruption. I can tell he wants to whisper all of the choice words—*hormones, premenstrual, girl things*—but to me he says, "I'm sorry. It was all a joke." He grips my hands in his. "Truce?"

THE MEN ARE talking in low cautious voices. They are talking about birdies and bogeys and woods and irons, which in many ways is the same conversation with different nouns. The women have sprung to action and have begun setting my dining table with crystal and silver and Wedgwood china, all wedding presents eighteen years ago. They are laughing now about things their children have said and done. They are talking about their perennial beds, knowing that soon enough I will have to join in. The peonies are just on the verge of bursting into full bloom and Joyce knows that next to the first breath of autumn this is my very favorite time of the year.

WHEN MY SON and I stood in front of the model of Lucy, it was as if the world stopped for just a second, just long enough for us to take note of how far we had come and how far we had to go. He waited until his classmates ran off in hysterical laughter and then—could he have sensed my great respect for this ancient little hominid?—took my hand and whispered, "I bet she was real pretty for her time." My heart leapt forward a couple of millennia. This boy, this future man, was evolution in action. I tell this story and the women all smile; they relax in a way that they haven't all night long. It begins a whole ring of conversation around topics of love and warmth, desire and longing. I am easily drawn into the circle but a part of me is still thinking about bare breasts and day-old coffee, empty bank accounts and biopsies, neglected children and scar tissue. I am thinking of Lucy as she limped her way to the water's edge seeking rest; I am thinking of her as she lay there millions of years ago staring out at this world for the very last time.

Cats

ABBOTT IS OUT there again and when Anne hears his feeble attempts with his key at a lock long changed, she freezes, holds her breath, hopes that this time something will occur to him, some glimpse of something will snap him back into present time and his life with the woman he left her for one April afternoon twelve years ago. The kitchen was blue then, Wedgwood blue, the place mats were straw, a wedding present from a friend in her college dorm, someone she hasn't seen since the day she married Abbott and everyone threw rice and blew kisses. As he told her the news "I'm leaving," she thought of the friend who'd given her the mats all those years ago, and about how she had no idea where she was living or what she was doing. How we let people slip from present to past, rarely looking back.

"Anne," he said. "Did you hear what I just said?"

She remembers nodding as he told her what she had been waiting to hear. There was someone else. Though, he added, the someone was not, of course, the reason he was leaving. Their marriage would be ending even if there weren't another woman. She wanted to ask a simple *then why?* but couldn't get the words up and over her tongue. Their sons had been at school and the noon sun streamed through the very window that had made her want to buy the house to begin with, a big bay window—big enough for hanging plants —casting a warm patch of light in the center of the room. The boys were eight and ten then, and when they got home that day, they found her sitting in the kitchen, a pile of unraveled straw on the table in front of her. They told her she looked just like the girl in "Rumpelstiltskin" and then they made awful faces and begged her to guess their names. She missed their big fat cat, who used to curl up in the sunshine and sleep through the day. She missed the ease with which she could pacify the boys when they were babies, how she had once had the power to make everything in their lives okay.

• • •

Now THE BOYS are twenty and twenty-two, both in college, both with girlfriends. Now the divorced CEO of the hospital where she works as a physical therapist occasionally shares her bed. He would move in if she invited him. He would marry her in a second if she gave him the go-ahead, and her friends all issue warnings that she better not keep him waiting too long, that he is bound to give up one of these days and find another house in which to take up residence. Everyone thinks she is holding out so that Abbott has to keep sending money. The new wife tells anyone who will listen how Anne is intentionally bleeding them dry. That's not true. Sometimes she isn't sure what is true.

THOUGH SHE LIVES on in the same house, she sleeps in a different room, an addition she worked and saved to build after Abbott had left and moved in across town and started a whole new family. Anne herself had been the new younger wife and the newest was even younger.

SHE TURNED THEIR old bedroom into a rumpus room and let it evolve along with the boys: puppet theater and LEGO blocks, pool table and stereo speakers. She painted it azure; they painted it black. And during each incarnation she remained aware of its original status; her mind never released the position of the bed, the way the light bathed the room in the late afternoon, a time they had often—whenever life permitted—allowed themselves the luxury of a nap. It was during those times she felt—if only for a second—the satisfied reassurance that she had made no mistake when she agreed to marry him.

People from far away who loved her began calling as soon as word reached them that Abbott had left. They called to say *come home come home*, and she was tempted. The home of her childhood was waiting just a few hours down the interstate. Sometimes at night she got herself to sleep picturing the town—flatland and tobacco barns, billboards calling her to the coast. She thought of those summer nights when she was a kid and had nothing to do but ride her bike through the streets of her hometown.

But by then home needed to be where her children were at home. Home had become the Japanese maple she planted when they bought the house and the roses she had trained up a trellis by the garage. So she had changed what she could afford to change. The sheets. The paint. She adopted a kind old yellow Lab to replace the cat in their marriage, Possum, on whom she had completely doted until Abbott was ready to have a child. The cat's death, twelve years after their wedding, coincided with Abbott's straying, and the two events were forever linked in her mind. The old Lab lived long enough to help her through the transition.

"Probably coyote or raccoon chow," he had said and shaken his head as she and the children wept over Possum's disappearance. "After twelve years, old Possum is nothing but a cheap lunch."

That comment and the scent on his face and neck when he came home from God knows where—he said golf, he said baseball, he said auto show, places she never went with him—told her that he was not who she had thought he was. He had become a stranger. This was what she was thinking as she picked her way through the wooded strip of land that separated their yard from the yards of yet another new neighborhood. In these woods the wild creatures had their own lairs, their own food supply. She could feel them watching her from their dark holes and caves as they waited for night to fall. That there had been no sign of Possum had made her feel hopeful even though deep down she knew better.

AND NOW ABBOTT is back, twisting and turning the knob with his own persistent optimism. She dries her hands and opens the door to his tired bewildered face. His wife always comes to lead him away like a confused child. Her appearance, however fraught with anger and frustration, seems to call him back into his present life, but until she shows up, he is back in their marriage. He asks where the boys are. He leans in and kisses her lips, pulls her close before she can catch her breath and step aside. He picks up on a conversation they had over a dozen years ago. How he's thinking about opening his own business. How he's thinking he should buy all the little drive-through buildings left behind by a defunct bank. How he will stock them with late-night necessities: milk and aspirin, diapers and toilet paper, beer and tampons. Twenty-four-hour service. Drive right through. People don't have to get dressed; they don't have to lift the baby out of the car. WHATEVER GETS YOU THROUGH THE NIGHT. The slogan was hers. The dream was his, one of fast fortune. There were many nights when she was all alone and believed more than ever that they had devised a brilliant plan. Necessities: those wee hours of the morning when a kid's fever spiked and not a drop of Tylenol in the house, or times when she realized that there would be no milk for her morning coffee.

IN ALL THE years since Abbott left, Anne has not slept a whole night through. Usually she wakes at two, sometimes three. Even with her CEO lying beside her, she often can't keep herself from playing through the nights she lay

there with Abbott, the tension between them so thick she
felt she might strangle on it, so thick it forced her awake,
the beginnings of the chronic habit. There is a time in a
woman's life when being a mother may be all that she can
successfully be, with her mind so fragmented by thoughts of
fevers and stitches and homework and Little League. Laundry and cleaning, shopping and cooking. A bath is a luxury.
Sleep, the greatest luxury of all. He kept commenting on
how she had changed. She knew what was going on was
what had changed. She could almost pinpoint the day he
came home with a different look about him. She could smell
the deception, but she didn't have proof. Night after night,
she had lain beside him wanting anything he could give her:
a confession, an apology, a profession of his love even with
an admission of his inability to remain faithful. Now she
hated the part of herself that over the years still refused to let
go of a love that he refused to return. She hated the part of
herself that delighted in the fate of the young unencumbered
women that so many men who stray manage to find. A year,
maybe two and then *that* woman is also encumbered, only
this time he has someone who is too young to share his
memories. She was disgusted with the part of herself that
pictured Abbott in such a state of aloneness.

Her great-aunt Rosemary was fond of saying that by and

large marriage is an unnatural state. Anne resisted the notion and clung to the natural history of certain rare monogamous creatures in the wild—the prairie vole, the purple martin, geese—even while she secretly believed Rosemary was probably right. Why else do women so easily settle in with their litters and nests; why do the females in nature blend into the background while the males remain flashy and continue life as sexual predators? Why was man created to continue giving life while women ran out of time, ran out of eggs?

I am dispensable, she thought one night when the coyotes' blood-chilling cries kept her awake. *A temporary shelter, a brief stop on a very long journey.*

Now SHE SLIPS the cordless phone into her pocket and goes into the bathroom to call Abbott's wife while he murmurs to himself about how great everything looks, how neat and clean. She closes the bathroom door, leaving just enough of a crack that she can see his shadow, hear his footsteps. She plans to once again whisper into the receiver *He's here, I have him,* but then there is no answer, and his voice— strong and coherent—on the answering machine startles her and she hangs up.

OVER A YEAR ago, her sons had told her there were problems. At first they thought he had had a stroke of some kind. Then a brain tumor. There had been a CAT scan, all kinds of tests. He was just that unlucky person, a man barely sixty in the throes of dementia.

"But isn't he too young for this?" she had asked his young wife.

"Yes," she said, her eyes lined and weary. Their children—a boy and a girl—were barely in junior high.

"And *I'm* too young for this," the wife added, then she caught herself and softened. She spoke then as if reciting from a medical textbook, spoke of her support group and how most of the others were a lot older and yet it did happen. One in a zillion. "Lucky huh?" she asked. "And think about genetics, will you? Your children and my children." She said all of this with Abbott right there in the next room. She said, "*your* children and *my* children," the business of women.

"I'LL BE THERE soon," the wife had said last time. She hesitated. "Maybe if you stopped letting him in . . ."

But he might get lost. He might get hit by a car. He might get mugged, she wanted to say.

When Anne was a child her great-aunt Rosemary had had a cat who wandered, a gigantic yellow-and-white tom named Pumpkin Pie who regularly came home beaten and battered. Nobody got their male cats fixed back then. They were allowed to go about their business, spraying and screwing and prowling the streets. Everyone in the neighborhood knew Pumpkin Pie by name. They would feed and pet him; sometimes in the winter he'd be invited in to snooze by a fire. Sometimes the call of nature and a female cat in heat was more than he could bear and some well-intentioned neighbor would have to turn a hose on him. Rosemary painted his battle wounds with Mercurochrome, bright orange splotches on his silky white fur. In winter, Pumpkin Pie liked to climb up and snuggle down near the engine of a recently driven car. But one night he wound up riding all the way across town. When he climbed out and ran away, Anne's great-uncle, a man too old for running, tried to follow and catch him. In vain. They mourned and blamed one another; Rosemary locked herself in the bathroom and sobbed. Then three weeks to the day, there he was again, clawing on the screen door and crying, one ear ripped and bleeding.

"Marriage goes against nature," Rosemary had said. She sat stroking the big tom, the white of his throat bright orange with Mercurochrome. "The tom wants to roam while the missus stays home with the little ones until they pull her old teats to death. Then she just wants to stay home. I myself have always just wanted to stay at home."

ANNE HAD TOLD the boys about Pumpkin Pie and his trip across town, stoking any lingering hopes that Possum had met a similar fate, or that some well-meaning neighbor had let her in and would soon read her tag and call to say that she was fine. "Unless she lost her tag," Abbott added, giving all three of them hard leveled stares. "Then we may never learn what happened. If so, it can't be helped. It can't be changed."

He was right, of course. It could have been an animal, could have been a car. Anyway, someone was nice enough to take the body to a veterinarian. They had her in the freezer if Anne would like to come and claim the body. They had some Polaroids so she could make a positive ID; the tag was close by but not on the cat's neck at the time it was found. They strongly advised that she not look at the body. "Better to remember her as she was," the teenage attendant recited handing Anne the box.

She built Possum a little mausoleum, easy enough on that frigid February afternoon. A little spit for mortar and the bricks froze solid. Without ever looking under the wrappings, she put the body into her biggest Tupperware and sealed the lid; she could not stand the thought of some hungry creature digging up what little bit remained. And then she just sat there. Anne had a lot in common with Possum. Black hair with the occasional streak of gray, voluntary sterilization. (She liked to believe that this is what Possum—at least in those later years—would have chosen for herself as well.) They both appreciated fine wool fabrics and warm spots in front of windows.

She had put the Tupperware down into the little brick cave just as Abbott was about to go out that dark late afternoon. His breath formed a cloud as he called out to her. He had a dinner meeting, hoped it wouldn't go on too long, but he never knew. He was wearing a new shirt, a shade of green that brought out the green of his eyes. She'd bought him a sweater that shade one Christmas that he had refused to wear, clinging staunchly to a wardrobe of khaki and navy, the occasional burgundy or gray. "Men don't wear this kind of color," he'd said. She thought about that as she watched him drive away. *Men don't primp and preen and wear that kind of color unless there is someone new out there asking for it, someone waiting for a sign.*

By that springtime afternoon when he broke the news in

the kitchen, she was almost relieved, she had waited so long for him to tell her the truth. Anything is better than the waiting, she told herself as she stared out the window where Possum's brick tomb had thawed and toppled to one side. And after he left with most of his personal belongings already piled on the backseat of his car, and before the boys got home, she did what she was not supposed to do. She looked. She peeled back the soggy layers of towel and stared down at what had once been Possum. There was absolutely nothing familiar left.

EVERY TIME THE wife came after him, her eyes seemed to say *This is supposed to be your life.* Did her eyes also say *Do you want him back?*

The wife looked all around Anne's house, maybe looking for old traces of her husband, or maybe in awe of the order a single woman with grown children can bring to a home. A calm. A peacefulness. The wife was drawn to a framed photograph of Anne and her CEO and then to a small picture of Anne and Abbott at the beach with the boys—a picture taken three years before the end; it was the one photo of him that she had never managed to put away. It reminded her of a time when trust and faith meant everything.

But today, Anne lets time pass before calling again.

Abbott is standing in the doorway of her room looking at the bed.

"Okay," he finally says. "Something's different."

"No," she says, "nothing's changed."

"C'mon, you can say." He goes and stands by the window. "Anne?" He calls her name as if testing it over his tongue, then repeats it. "Anne, how many years . . ." he pauses, shakes his head.

"Since we moved in?" she asks, and he nods, still clearly unsure of his question.

"Almost twenty years," she answers him. It's not a lie.

"It's good." He leans his face against the glass pane. His shoulders are slightly hunched, thinner than she remembers, his corduroys loose through the hips.

"Yes, I think so, too." She goes and puts her arm around his waist and he returns the gesture while still staring out at the small backyard. In a few minutes she really will have to call his wife. She may already be driving over, frantic and worried, just blocks away, coming once again to claim him. But for now Anne can't seem to move away from the warm afternoon light that fills her room.

"Here, lie down." She leads him over to the bed and then stretches out beside him. When he rolls over to take her in his arms, she sees the change in his eyes, faint traces of what she once knew. He pulls her closer, burying his face in her neck, his breath warm, his heart beating against her chest. Same heart. Same rhythm. It is the most natural thing in the world.

"Rest," she whispers, her hand stroking the hair back from his forehead, then slowly moving to the warmth of his neck. She moves her hand down his back and then inches her fingers under his belt and along the edge of his pants, teasing only to then pop the elastic of his boxers. It was an old joke; it was *their* old joke and her need to repeat it seems an involuntary act, one that makes him laugh and hug her tighter. And then in the very next second, he is on the verge of crying. "What will we do now?" he asks and shakes his head, a look of total defeat washing over him. "What can we do?"

"Rest," she says. "Just rest." She waits for him to close his eyes and for his breath to fall into the rhythm of sleep, his fingers still linked through her own. She knows she needs to call. She knows he is not hers to keep even though she would like nothing better than to believe that at the end of his long journey, after all was said and done, that what he wanted more than anything in the world was to come home.

Dogs

IF I WERE a dog I would have been put down by now. Put down. Euthanized. Sent to the country (the euphamized euthanized). Gassed.

I once dated a boy who had the nickname Mad Dog, but it was because he loved his wine, and what an unsophisticated drinker he was: Ripple, Boone's Farm, T. J. Swann, Mogen David—MD 20 20 some called it—he called it Mad Dog. But that was long before I thought of myself as a mad dog. I dated Mad Dog over five years ago when I was in high school and had my whole life ahead of me. He was back before the mistake of my two-month marriage to an ice sculptor who left as soon as I got pregnant, saying he was sorry but that his profession required a lot of concentration and focus.

That mistake was back when my friend Marissa took on the notion of her superior wisdom and when I might have been described as a well-tuned instrument, physically and mentally. I could play a concerto and I could also flat-out fiddle, but then my strings got wound so tight that they started popping all over the place and making a mess. Thank the good Lord my baby, Richie, was smarter than his father. That child, even before birth, became my lifeline, my reason for working hard to establish my own business. There are people who tell me that I have become a nicer person since having Richie and since working with the dogs. They don't say if this is the result of Richie or of canine companionship or some combination of the two.

I don't mean to imply that I'm rabid. Rather, I am of the frightened aggressive variety of mad dog. The type is well known to animal behaviorists. I will bite you before you bite me. I am like the dog that even the dog psychiatrists can't cure. They might try Prozac. They might even try a muzzle, but I can bite through steel when I take on a mood. Woody (with whom I was involved, I am ashamed to say) discovered this about me fairly early on. When he first hired me at the Dog House he said he liked a challenge. He said he could train me without breaking my spunk. (I wasn't sure if he was teasing or not.) He slapped me on my butt when he said this and he said it in front of a whole roomful of clients sitting there with their little charges on their laps or at their feet. And of course I knew he had a lot more in mind for me than pulling off ticks or treating some retriever's pernicious ear infection or hosing down the concrete runs out back. I'm sorry to say I smelled the desire on him and I do have to also say that at first meeting I was kind of turned on. Let's just say if you've never gotten right up in a pit bull's face, you might be curious.

I should explain. I am in the boarding and grooming business and I had plenty of work experience, mainly with dogs, long before I took up with Woody. I once accidentally killed a cat by giving it a dog flea dip (poisonous, I now know, to felines) and have the irrational belief that cats everywhere have heard that news and are ready to make me pay. So, I am known as the Dog Girl, a title I take great pride in. I do good work, and trust me, it isn't always easy. For instance, those little hairless breeds get blackheads. I have one Chinese crested client I call Miss Clearasil (not in front of her owner, of course) and a Westie with eczema I call Little Leper. There is a Labrador who passes a big white tube sock each and every time he comes in for a visit. His owner, an elderly woman with a hearing problem, was so ashamed when I told her that Ellery appeared to be eating up her husband's socks she cried. Her distress, however, has not curbed Ellery's appetite.

This establishment—the Dog House—is, along with Richie, my life. I am stashing money away, and all the while building up a clientele that would follow me when I am able to move on. I favor the pair of basenjis who come in once a month for a little weekend visit while their owners—a good-looking couple who drive up in a convertible, their overnight bags already on the backseat—take a romantic trip. I used to say to Woody, "Wouldn't that be wonderful?" and he said, "What, and leave all this luxury behind?"

You can imagine what my line of work smells like. When I get home at night, I leave my clothes and sneakers outside on the deck to air out. Woody has said "I like how you smell, Dog Girl" many times. The first time he said it, I liked it, but it's gotten old. Now I'd like to smell like the basenji owner. Her long hair carries the medley fragrance of oils and lotions as if she lived in the cosmetic section of a department store. Do you know basenjis are nearly mute? Instead of barking, they make a little chuckle sound deep in their throats, which makes me sad, but the skills they lack in the vocal chords are more than compensated for in their agile little paws. I have seen that pair scale an eight-foot chain-link fence in ten seconds flat and escape. An admirable talent, I think.

I CONSIDER MYSELF a New Age survivalist. I do some yoga and ingest a little Saint John's every now and again. I have some crystals and my astrological chart and a book on feng shui. I have everything I might need to survive a crisis—batteries, water, freeze-dried entrees—everything but a firearm. I don't believe in firearms even though Woody tried to frighten me into getting a tiny purse pistol. What he really wanted, I think, was to scare me into letting him move in and live here. I refused that. I did *not* want to repeat the ice sculptor affair. I would wait and decide when I saw where our relationship was headed. It didn't take me long to understand where he wanted the relationship to go. He was not interested in the tête-à-tête so much as the crotch-à-crotch. There were some days I believed I might have to turn a hose on him just as I often have to do when we are boarding a large-breed bitch in heat. Some dogs leave me no other choice.

"I worry about you, Dog Girl," Woody whispered and pinched my breast with no respect whatsoever for Richie, who was asleep right there in a Snugli strapped to my chest. "Bad things happen to women who are all alone in the world."

"Well I don't believe in firearms," I told him and flicked his wandering hand off me. "I tell you what I do believe in though." He waited for me to finish, his hand poised and ready to strike again. It is a shame how much cuter he is than he is smart, but that happens. You see that in quite a few breeds.

"For protection, I believe in dogs and baseball bats," I told Woody. "If you come in here uninvited I'm prepared to beat you and to ask the dogs to assist me in handling the situation." I told Woody that again after the collie incident, and that time he didn't laugh because I had a Louisville Slugger in my right hand and the leash of a mistreated Akita in the other. I like to think I gave him fair warning.

PETS ARE OFTEN a good way to keep unwanted guests away. Dogs. Snakes. Cats presenting half a bird or mouse, a squirrel entrail. Birds who fly around and relieve themselves at will. All of them are a positive force if you don't wish visitors. That's what I told Woody. But his heart was not at all in the business. I don't believe he even likes animals but bought into the Dog House only in hopes of earning more than his fair share of the almighty dollar. Woody is probably one of those boys who kick at a dog if it runs up beside their bikes; he is probably one of those who try to run over cats with lawn mowers. I prayed that Richie would have no memory of Woody there in my bed in his bikini underwear.

I said to myself, "When Woody leaves I'll replace him pound for pound with *dog*." I had no respect whatsoever for him. When he moved out I got myself a little shepherd mix and a Great Dane. Bubba and Bjorn. They weight the bed just right. And my little papillon, Princess, accounts for the five-pound fluctuation Woody got on the weekends from pizza and those creme horns he loves. Princess likes to doze up on Bjorn's great big head like a little hair ornament. It tickles Richie to death to see them there like that. They are his family.

MARISSA, OF ALL PEOPLE, has said to me recently, "Why don't you grow up? You have a child to tend to." She said, "Adults don't have a house full of pets."

I said, "Well, Marissa, I don't know that my habits are worse than yours—faking every bad illness known to man in hopes of meeting a doctor." I wanted to remind her that I was there in junior high all those times she accidentally on purpose spilled a Kotex from her purse so boys would think of her as a *woman*. But I held my tongue. Friends cannot say everything they're thinking.

I said, "I *am* a grown-up, Marissa. I have a child to raise on my own. I have a profession, a calling. I have a *career*. And it just so happens that what I always wanted in life was relationships with dogs of all sizes and shapes and colors. A whole universe that I could teach to get along with one another, share, be family. I've done that. If only the world could take note." I said, "Tell me why your obsession with antibiotics and the cataloging of diseases you always think you might have is a better calling."

"My sensitive medical issues are not a calling, as you so weirdly call it," she said. "I am a professional designer, which is a grown-up thing, unlike you always talking about the Westie's eczema or those wrinkled dogs' respiratory problems. That is not a grown-up thing." Marissa got red in the face. "And neither is marrying an ice sculptor."

"Well, he was one of the very best ice sculptors around," I said. "He once did a swan for the Hyatt Regency in Atlanta. Besides, I never claimed my marriage was a great thing but you know what? You know what?" I backed her into the corner and made her look at me. "Richie is a good thing. So which came first, the chicken or the egg?"

"I agree about Richie," she said and tried to move out of the corner but I wouldn't let her. We have known one another since elementary school and she knows that I can take her on and beat her with both hands tied behind my back if I need to.

"So I like dogs. So what?" I yelled. "What in the hell is wrong with the fact that I like to talk about different kinds of dogs the same way you like to talk about different kinds of chairs: *Here is a wing back. Thomas Jefferson sat here. And here is JFK's rocker, perfect for those going off of theirs. Oh yes, and here's the club chair like they use on all the late-night talk shows; the club chair is just what every little woman in Stepford needs so that when the man gets home she can lean back and say 'Heeeerrrreee's Johnny!'* "

"Will you stop?" She pushes me away, and I step back and let her go. She clicks down the hallway just exactly like a poodle all coiffed and painted up. What a bitch. I can look at a person and tell you immediately by looks and personality what breed that person would be. I don't think Marissa would be interested, though. But, for instance, I think if Marilyn Monroe had been a bitch she'd have been a yellow Lab. They'd have dressed her up like a poodle again and again but deep down she was definitely a Lab and who better for a Lab to hook up with than a fella with balls. And where has Joe DiMaggio gone? Dead. Like so many of the best dogs.

• • •

OTHER THAN MARISSA, I don't have a whole lot of people friends. Go figure. I'd like to suggest they stop their yapping and go for a good long walk. Chase after something other than their own tails. I wish I could tell them that their depressions and neuroses are simply the by-products of the wrong diet and training. Think of the fortitude it takes to eat and pass a man's tube sock. *Try that as a cathartic*, I want to say.

Woody had me wearing a choke for a couple of months there. The kind with spikes. Figuratively, of course, though if he could make a woman companion wear one legally he'd do that. He's got a woman right now that he jerks around any way that he pleases. Bless her heart, she looks like a Chinese crested with that poof of frizzy hair like a pom-pom and her bad complexion. And Woody? He wants to be a pit bull of a man but he is a Chihuahua.

He thinks I am hurt when he parades his little poochie past me. He believes I have separation anxiety. He doesn't know that I have saved enough to open my own little place and that I will soon be his fiercest competitor, that I will soon go public with the truth about the beautiful collie who died of old age and for whom Woody promised the family a proper burial complete with flowers and the dog's favorite squeak toy inside the lovely walnut box he billed them at a couple of hundred dollars. I will divulge this: how, while Woody, two hundred dollars the richer, was in his office with Miss Chinese Crested, I took a trash bag of dog hair down to the Dumpster only to discover the collie lying there, all awkward, stiffened limbs covered over with soiled newspapers from the kennels.

There's a lot I can forgive in the world but not that. I climbed down in there and pulled Bonny out, not an easy feat for a woman of my size, I'll tell you. I went and got the display coffin, the only dog coffin that Woody had in the place, and I lifted the heavy body up and into it, put it on a dolly, and rolled it out to the field behind the kennels and their runs. I spent the rest of the afternoon digging a grave and burying Bonny. I was sickened that such a beautiful life could ever be left to the hands of somebody as stupid and careless as Woody.

SOMETIMES WHEN I am feeling particularly mad— I'm stressed, I'm crazed, I'll bite your head off—I sit down and write myself a letter about how things will get better. I make out a list of what I should and should not do: do not bark and growl and flip off the crossing guard over at Richie's day care center—this will not get you anywhere; do sit right on the photos you took of the dead collie and the pictures you took of the kennel runs when Woody was in charge; do not breathe a word about how he has cheated on his income taxes for the past five years; do wait until it's time to let go of that tube sock you've swallowed. I tell myself, there is no shame in being a bitch in heat, no shame in wanting a litter.

As a matter of fact, I may read a few of my thoughts aloud to Marissa when she comes over, once again all heartbroken by some jerk who gave her a prescription for tetracycline at the end of a stormy night of sex and then never called her again. I will tell her that I understand how important chairs and sofas and tables are in her life and how I respect this; I will not leave dog hair on the velvet upholstery of her new Chippendale dining-room chairs and I will not let Richie teethe on their legs. And I will tell her that loyalty is more important than any house-decorating item, the kind of loyalty—though she might not want to hear it—that you usually only get from a good dog. The kind that you need from a good friend. I will say, *We want the same things, honey. You know we do.* I will tell her everybody—bitch and dog alike—has those days when all they can think about is a piece of tail, anal glands, teeth sinking into the soft flesh of the throat.

Marissa will raise her hand in disgust and say *I do not!* and I will once again have to explain that I am using a metaphor before I move forward to say how what we really want, each and every day, is for someone to be willing to throw some love our way so that we can retrieve it and return the favor. All we really want, I tell her, is for someone we really care about to say *Speak to me, girl, speak. Now stay.*

Toads

AMONG THE THINGS my mother left me when she died much too young of cancer were the engagement ring my father gave her at a college football game when they were both nineteen, her mother's prized mink cape sealed for decades in a plastic zipper bag with mothballs, a framed daisy made of her grandmother's hair, and my stepfather, James T. Allen, who came complete with my mother's handwritten instructions as if he were some kind of fragile orchid who needed this much light, this much water, and this much vodka at the end of the day.

James T. Allen had no children of his own and has certainly never considered me one, either. I didn't even know what the T in his name stood for and—I'm embarrassed to say—my husband and kids and I have had many hours of fun coming up with possibilities. Tanless (contribution of my husband, Ron, avid golfer and sun worshiper); Tasteless and Toneless (I am the one who washes his beige polyester-blend belongings and listens to his rare monotonous utterings); Testosteroneless (from my oldest son, Sam, who at seventeen has enough to supply the whole state); and last but not least Turdo and Toadman (these from my ten year old, Matt, who spends much of his time flipping over rocks in search of the drab amphibians). It seems that most of our monikers, with the exception of Turdo and Toadman, have to do with what he isn't rather than what he is. Because what, after all, is he? If he were a piece of furniture in a showroom he would be the beige Naugahyde thing in the corner, not a chair, or a sofa, more like an ottoman. If he were a car he would be the beige Impala. If he were shoes he would be beige Hush Puppies. If you were to go out and flip over a rock, he is what you would find burrowed there. Actually, all of these are understatements.

Basically he sits in the corner staring first at the newspaper, which he sheds section by section onto the floor around him, and then at the television, always on the Headline News channel or the weather station. He talks to my husband about investments, which he finds mildly exciting since he'd been an investment broker, though he says he himself never invested in anything. He talks to Matt about the virtues of being a boy who picks up after his elders, nodding toward the sections of newspaper on the floor as an example of elder litter. Who knows what he would talk to Sam about; he never gets the chance. Sam has it all figured out— the escape—he simply stops in front of James T. Allen's chair, lifts one ear of his Walkman, cocks his head and says "check ya later," and he's off and running, laughter coursing through his veins. In private he whispers to me that James is the Zombie Dude; he is the Man Most Likely to Slip into a Coma—Man Who Most Resembles a Brussels Sprout—the Crash Dummy—Keeper of the Black Hole. These jokes have become our mother-and-son bondings of late, and though I sometimes feel guilty, I've done nothing to stop the game; we show our love for one another through our disdain for James.

JAMES WAS ONLY sixty-five when my mother died— a very old sixty-five—and I'm still not sure why it is that he lives with us. She died here and he couldn't think of anywhere else to go? Maybe. He needs help remembering when to take his different medicines? Maybe that was what my mother thought, but he has yet to even let me read the labels. His one and only outing of the month is going to the drugstore to fill all those prescriptions himself. Once a year he checks in with the doctor who writes the prescriptions. He keeps his pills locked in a little box by his bed.

I don't know what exactly is wrong with James. I asked my mother several times, more frequently as she was reaching the end and telling me how he needed lots of care. Her answer was *"Many many things* are a burden to James." "Such as?" I asked and she would conveniently doze off with a whispered murmur of "poor thing." Arthritis? Schizophrenia? Cancer? Could he have had a lobotomy in his youth?

If Poor Thing had any family they had apparently given up on him. He didn't get phone calls or mail. My mother had explained that James had focused for so long on his job that by age fifty he found himself with nothing else in his world. That my mother could be the spark plug in someone else's life was a shocker. I didn't push much beyond learning that James was an only child and that he was friendless because, according to my mother, a man in a powerful position (was he?) can't have friends. Nobody likes the boss.

To my knowledge the only friend he ever had was his former lawyer, an older gentleman who had been his neighbor for many years. James used to take the man a basket of fruit at Christmas but stopped when the old guy had a stroke that affected his memory and he moved into Turtle Bay Nursing Home. Sam said, "But you could still, like, take him something, right?" and James T. looked up, shook his head, and asked a bewildered "What for?"

"Oh I don't know," I offered. "Because you're such a kind and generous man?" He thanked me for the compliment apparently missing my sarcasm and making me feel really small.

MY MOTHER, WHO I believe willed herself to die (if such a thing is really possible), also told me that James had "terrible digestive flow." Exactly what that meant, I don't know. What I do know is that he makes noises inside his mouth and chest cavity that sound like a host of demons trying to burst free. Burps and sucks and smacks, the kinds of sounds that leave a listener who's trying to tend to her own business jerking and snapping with mini-Tourette's. I sometimes find myself thinking that if he dared to open wide that cavernous mouth he would emit, like Pandora's box, all the uglies of the world—a swarm of flies, locusts, the river Styx pouring forth in projectile vomit. But no. He opens only a crack, he smacks, he sucks his gums. He says, "You're low on milk." He says, "The TV reception is not good when you run the hair dryer." He says, "I'm in need of Metamucil."

"Thank you," I say. "Are you through watching Headline News now?" Wouldn't you like to take a walk? Call a friend? Ride a bike? Find a pulse?

He is stationary.

He doesn't want to do anything at all.

He is *so* stationary, Ron says we could start using him as a clothes rack. We could rent him out to the circle of widows in our neighborhood as the Fake Man, like the thing we saw an ad for in a magazine not long ago. You can put the Fake Man by a window, or let him ride in your passenger seat. You would never ever feel alone with Fake Man by your side. For a more realistic effect, put a beige hat on him.

I HAVE TO find myself some ways to handle the anger I feel toward my mother for leaving me this boring ottoman of a man. I am, I realize, as angry as I was when my parents separated. My dad left and I couldn't get as mad at him as I wanted to because, even at fifteen, there was a part of me that understood why he left. To outsiders (even to my older brother) he was the bad guy and she was the helpless defenseless martyr. I suspected this was what she had wanted all along. She wanted a good reason why she was so miserable, which she hadn't had when she had a handsome, successful husband—a prince—and pretty good kids and a great house and a big circle of friends. She couldn't do the happy thing. Or the healthy thing. She would much rather have been the victim and to die that way than to be a survivor who must hop to and get up off of her ass and *do something*.

When I say this sort of thing, I get looks of horror from friends and from my brother in California, who I might add did *not* inherit James T. Allen and has nothing to worry about but himself and his partner and the little Jack Russell they all but keep in a bassinet. Even Ron says I am sexist and unfair not to side with my mother. He says, "Sure your dad's a great guy but he's not perfect. He is human. Why do you believe that's what she wanted? Give me one good reason?"

And I can give him two. First of all, the woman my mother claims my father left us for—he gave her the woman's name and address and phone number—did not exist. My mother was perfectly willing to accept this name and address and number and sigh, shake her head, cry into the telephone to friends who promised to bring her casseroles and do her errands for her. I was only fifteen, but I knew better. I called the number—help line. I rode my bike across town to the address—psychiatric practice. I scoured the phone book and later the courthouse records for the name we'd been given. And lo and behold, it turned out that Theda R. Dunster had never existed, at least not in this part of the world. I told my mother that none of it was true. I said, "Don't you see? This is a test." But evidently she didn't see or did not want to see and she failed the test. No retakes.

When I told my dad that I knew the truth, he made no admission, just smiled and hugged me up to his big chest. He whispered as we stood that way that he had tried everything he knew to do. That my mother was the person he had always wanted to live with. I waited then, holding my breath, knowing the answer was coming. "*Live* is the key word, honey," he said. "I'm too young to simply stop living." And I knew what he meant. He wasn't talking *fast* living. He was talking just ordinary living. Watch and comment on the sun either coming up or going down. Acknowledge the seasons as they pass. Laugh. Tell stories. Refuse to hunker down in a dark depression.

MY MOTHER MET Mr. Allen (as she referred to him for the first two months of their courtship) at a gas station out on the service road while they both waited in its smelly little glassed-in room while their cars got fixed up. I have tried to imagine them there, to imagine what they might have said to one another beyond *flat tire* and *oil change*. Maybe they recognized in each other the distaste for anything that could be flashy or fun about a car. Maybe finding another utilitarian, boring creature got them excited: My car is white—good visibility and cool enough not to install air-conditioning. *Mine, too!* I do not have a stereo, nor do I want such frivolity. *Neither do I.* I removed the cigarette lighter so that no one would ever smoke and risk burning the seat. *What a great idea!* Are you as opposed to bumper stickers as I am? *Oh, yes, yes, yes!*

I acted out my little skit for Ron and the boys when we were in the car driving to the beach for the weekend. We spent the whole wonderful day imagining what James T. Allen did in our house when he was there by himself. We pictured him ripping off his glasses the way the old mousy-secretary routine used to go and morphing into a wild and groovy swinging-singles type. But then we got more realistic and we imagined him peeking into everyone's drawers or, if he got really daring, watching a television sitcom.

I TOLD RON that my second and even better reason to believe my father's story is that he only started dating af-ter my mother began spending all of her time with James Allen and because my dad always dated women his own age. He could easily have survived and excelled in a much younger world but he chose to (after my mother took the step first) marry Margaret, a livelier, Technicolor version of what he had left behind. As hard as it has been for even me—their daughter—to believe, it is clear that my mother was his first choice. And her choice of James Allen over my father is a choice equal to choosing a hysterectomy/toenail removal/root canal over a trip to Bermuda.

MY DAD HAS aged nicely. He's handsome. He's charming. Tan face and arms. Keeps his golf gear in the trunk of his car. He has all kinds of projects. Birdhouses and bonsai. He loves the Marx brothers and Abbott and Costello. He loves to cook, especially Tex-Mex. He likes to camp out, even now, and will take the grandchildren (he has mine plus three little girls compliments of Margaret's daughter), who adore him, to the vacant lot in his neighborhood, pitch a tent, build a fire, sing songs, tell the same old stories he used to tell us—stories all set right there in the neighborhood and designed to scare you silly. He is definitely alive. I see Margaret's daughter (a woman exactly my age) cling to him with awe, this father she always dreamed was out there. No, he's not perfect. He is sloppy and sometimes so engrossed in a subject that he can't talk or think about anything else. Margaret stands behind him and rolls her eyes, flaps her hands in imitation of his endless hyper chatter. But at least he's there; he's real. Which is what I am forever saying to my mother in my head.

"I'VE BEEN THINKING," James says one day, which in and of itself is quite exceptional, "you need to alphabetize your books."

"Go for it," I say.

"Oh, I didn't mean I'd do it." He emphasizes "I'd" as if I suggested he run out into the yard naked. "That's a rainy-day project for you." His mind slips no more than is probably normal. He seems reasonably healthy beyond the top-secret digestive troubles and the shadowy burdens of life. I make up ways to make myself tolerant of his immobility. I pretend he is a quadriplegic.

"I need some water," he says. "Not too cold though, it makes my belly hurt." I hand him the water and then ask if he can help me gather up the newspapers around him for recycling but he doesn't budge. He has an aching belly. He is killing me.

I pretend he is a deaf quadriplegic.

I like to think my mother had regrets. Like at my wedding, where she and James sat on one side and my dad and Margaret on the other. I like to think my parents looked longingly across the aisle at one another. My wedding was in

the very church where my brother and I had been chris-
tened, the very one where I threw up in the vestibule one
awful rainy Sunday, a moment so memorable that my brother
and close friends from home will still say, "Remember when
you vomited in the vestibule?" And I will say, "Yes, at the
Hanging of the Greens service."

But what I remember best is being lifted up by my father
and carried out into the cool wet day, put down on the
backseat of our old Chevrolet and smelling tobacco and my
mother's perfume on the vinyl. She wore Shalimar then; he
never let her run out of it. And he sent her to get some wet
paper towels for my forehead and though she resisted at
first, though she worried about missing the service, *What
would people say? Could they really leave my brother in the
church to sit all by himself?* she did as he said. Somehow my
father was able to convince her that it was just fine to sit
there with us in the pouring-down rain. He talked about
priorities and the upcoming holidays. He would have
described at greater length the famous stuffing his grandmother used in the center of a crown pork roast if the first
mention of butter and meat and prunes hadn't made me
moan and gag. And when I got sick again, he swung open
the back door and eased me out onto the curb. He squatted
down beside me, his suit spattered with mud and throw up,

while my mother leaned out of the car and held my hair back from my face.

"Teamwork, love," he said to her then and smiled. "Great teamwork." And they laughed, their cold wet hands entwined on my sweaty neck. It is one of my very favorite memories.

I like to picture my parents at the college football game where my father proposed. Charlie "Choo Choo" Justice was the star player on the field; the marching band played the fight song. There were no lights in the stadium. The donation that built the stadium specified that it not accommodate anything taller than the trees. The university would have to wait many years before there could be night games. So it was the afternoon, autumn, sweater weather. Young men were swigging liquor from flasks; their girlfriends were wearing little white socks and loafers. I imagine my dad as one of the louder guys, cheering and laughing, I imagine that he mistook my mother's silence as shyness, a little bird in need of a few flight lessons. I think that he imagined far more longing and desire in her than actually existed. I marvel at what we all manage to make out of nothing, time and time again. And then he gave her the ring, slipped it onto her finger so quietly, easily, then squeezed so tightly it brought tears to her eyes.

"He almost broke my finger," she once said, interrupting his story as we drove to a family vacation.

"She was moved to tears," he said and laughed. And then later added, "She often is, isn't she?"

The day my father actually moved out, my mother and I sat studying the daisy picture that her grandmother had fashioned out of hair. My mother explained that this was something her grandmother said was trendy in the Victorian era —an art form of sorts. *Craft* better described what we had before us—a misshapen daisy made from a poor old woman's wiry, tangled hair. My dad had been gone for over an hour and still we studied it, the frame on the center of her bed, where we sat and waited for my brother to get home from his tennis lesson. We studied its petals as if they were tea leaves

"I think she must have been a sad woman," my mother said then, tracing a finger over the glass. "I think she probably always knew that she needed to make herself get up and move but something kept her from doing it."

"I thought she couldn't walk," I said then, still with a hopeful ear listening for the return of my dad. "I thought she was completely bed-bound when she made this and that was the whole story, that she got bored and began cutting off her hair, strand by strand."

"Yes, that's right," my mother said. I was hoping she would continue with the story about how the old demented woman got it in her mind to count all of the hairs on her head since they were indeed numbered. How she did he loves me, he loves me not, snipping and counting and then scribbling a number on the inside pages of the Bible by her bed. When she had enough hairs collected to braid a thin string, she began twisting oddly shaped petals and stems. I wanted to hear more about her dementia and how she, there at the end of her life, had in her mind that her husband, who was still very much alive and shuffling about the old country house, was already dead and had been found that way "nekked" in another's bed. My mother had told the story many, many times. She used a perfect country dialect to deliver the vulgarities the old woman tossed at the man she had lived with for fifty years. The family favorite was when she called him "dirty hog dick" in the presence of the pastor. My mother remembered being a child and standing in the doorway while her grandmother cursed and muttered "nekked, nekked I say," her hair half-shorn, ragged and stringy.

My mother told this story well. My father got excited, watching and listening. He would encourage her to tell it again and again; he praised her wonderful dialect and sense of humor. He begged her to tell it on holidays and to new friends. He said, "When you're old and sick are you going to turn on me that way?"

She said, "Only if I find you *nekked* in somebody else's bed."

Finally, as we sat studying the picture, my mother bent forward and began to cry. She said that the end of the story was that when the poor old woman finally got down to the last few pathetic strands, she stopped on "he loves me not," and even though her pitiful husband sat right there in front of her in the flesh and begged and pleaded and told her he loved her, there was no getting through.

Now JAMES T. ALLEN sits in front of my great-grandmother's hair daisy. "I guess you know all about this, huh?" I ask.

"No," he says. "What is it?"

"A daisy."

"Huh."

"Made of hair."

"Okay."

It is clear that I am interrupting his day of absolute boredom. Just this morning, I passed the open bathroom to see Sam standing there, a towel around his lean waist as he shaved, and I marveled that he was here in this house, with his parents still together, his parents still in love. Because of his happiness, he might never have reason to look as deeply into my life, or into Ron's. We might be dead before he sees us in the clear way I now see my father. He turned and gave me a look as if to say *Yeah? What do you want?* but then leaned close, mouthwash on his breath, hair slicked back the way his girlfriend recently suggested. "Why," he whispered, "doesn't James order the vegetable plate?"

I shrugged and he broke into snorts and giggles. He might as well have been nine. "Because he *is* the vegetable plate!" He was so tickled with himself, he had to sit down on the edge of the tub. "I mean, I don't mean to be mean," he gasped, "but he *is* the vegetable plate."

I wonder what he and my mother *did* talk about? Did my mother save her one story like a gem tucked away and protected or did she give it to this zombie who simply paid no attention and does not now remember. Or did my mother choose silence? A chance to slip beneath the fabric of life my dad had sewn with such a flair?

These questions become an obsession and one day I can't resist. As the sun begins to sink, before Ron and the kids get home, I mix James his habitual vodka and orange juice and I mix one for myself and just as the sunlight fades completely, before I reach to flick on the lamp, I say, "So what did you and Mom talk about when you sat together at this time of day?" After a long pause, after a long sip, he sighs and looks away. "I don't know," he says. "Maybe the news, what to have for dinner. You know," he glances at me and then fixes his gaze on the daisy, "I really don't remember."

He remains silent for what seems an eternity. I can hear my neighbor's sprinklers rotating; I hear him draw in a deep breath and sigh again. "All of our conversations run together," he says, without looking away from the wall. "Even at the very end we didn't say a whole lot." This is the most I have ever heard him say at once, and there is something in the sadness of his voice that makes me want to press the stop button, erase my question, put a lid on Pandora's box.

"I wanted her to talk more," he continues, "I did. I thought maybe there were things she needed to say. There were things I would have said back." He closes his eyes and rests his head on the back of the chair. I want to tell him that I wanted her to say things to me as well, but before I can push myself in that direction, he continues. "Emma had a lot to say when she was dying."

I jump with the mention of this new name. My mother had always referred to him as a widower, never making any mention of his first wife. "Emma and I had a lot to say to each other but then we had a lot of years between us." He smiles when he says her name, and there is a look of comfort on his face, something that I have not seen there before. His eyes are still closed and I can only imagine that he is picturing some bit of his life with Emma. "You must know by now," his voice shakes, "your mother was not a happy woman." He sits up straight with this statement and looks me in the eye. "I thought that once we were married and settled in our own world that it would all get better; I thought she was just sort of worried about how I would fit in." He waits as if wanting me to intervene. "It was easier for her to stay unhappy, that's all." He nods and I nod along with him. "I'd say, 'What can I do? Just tell me,' but she never did."

He fidgets, his right hand smoothing the brushed corduroy of the arm of the chair. My plan to have a good story to tell Sam and Ron late tonight has backfired. It is true that James T. Allen was my mother's white noise, her third martini, Demerol in her veins. It is true that his presence enabled her to check out of the world without anyone noticing her absence or her inability to change. He played the part my father was not willing to play. But what I didn't know, what I never even considered, is that James T. Allen never wanted the role she assigned him. Whether or not it was her conscious intention, she used him. In his own weak and watered-down way, he wanted exactly what my father had wanted. He wanted life. And now I understand, as he reaches for my hand, that this is where we come in.

Monkeys

EVERYBODY IN TOWN knew who Rommy Whitfield was. She was the woman with the monkey cage out on her front porch and a spider monkey named Mister Simmy inside it shaking the bars like a crazed convict and baring his sharp little yellow teeth. She was the woman with the most beautiful garden in town. She grew flowers and she grew vegetables. On late summer afternoons you would see her sitting in the glider on the shady end of her porch shelling field peas and butter beans into a big shiny colander on her lap.

Children came to spy on her, the mission being to creep close enough to hear the peas falling from their shells, close enough to hear what she was saying because her mouth was always moving, her head shaking from side to side. One boy had reported that she was cussing up a storm but he couldn't quite make out the words because Mister Simmy spotted him hiding in the shrubbery and started screeching and throwing his crap.

She knew the children came to look at her; a lot of adults who didn't know any better did, too. Her husband had killed himself. He had taken the sash from the silk robe he bought for her one Christmas and used it to hang himself. That was the attraction. They came to see what the woman who was married to the man who killed himself looked like. What was she doing there all alone with the monkey? Even people who had known her since she first came to town kept a somewhat cool distance after the death. Oh they came to the viewing down at the Cape Fear Mortuary and they came to the funeral; they whispered back and forth, speculating on *why* he had done this. Some of them knew things. That much was clear to Rommy sitting there in a hard metal chair and staring into the damp earth where Albert lay in his padded box. She could feel their tidbits of knowledge, their memories of this time or that, burning into her back. She kept her eyes open during the prayer, half hoping that Albert might rise up from the ground and break into hilarious laughter. He loved to trick people; he loved to go to birthday parties and pull coins from children's ears and flowers from his own sleeves. He loved to throw his voice so that it seemed as if Mister Simmy was singing "Red River Valley." Simmy would wear a little tiny cowboy hat strapped to his head and a bandanna around his neck so that he looked just like Albert. Yes, Albert loved nothing better than a trick. The fine art of deception.

ROMMY HAD LOTS of fruit trees heavy with fruit: apples and pears and hard sour cherries. She had a muscadine grapevine that had completely taken over the old car shed, where Albert used to sneak out for what he called his meditation. She knew he went out there to smoke a cigar, to think about life, and for the most part she resisted following him and trying to peek through the dark window at the rear of the shed. She planted the vine when they first got married and Albert promised to build her an arbor. They would have a wrought-iron café table and chairs in its shade. She had in mind that years in the future they would eat supper there on summer nights under the canopy of grapes. Sleep, creep, leap. That's what folks say about a vine and sure enough by the third year that grapevine had taken off in every direction.

But her prizes were her pomegranate bushes. They were big and robust and, come fall, they drooped low with their heavy red fruit. That was the fruit children most liked to sneak in and steal, because it was the rarest, with those little red seeds like rubies and the kind of sharp bitter juice that a child cannot resist. For a long time she wished that the children would just come on up and ask her for some fruit, let her go in and get them some iced tea and johnnycakes. One Halloween she had a bushel basket of pomegranates by the front door to hand out to the trick-or-treaters but they all managed to run past her house without looking. The ones that stopped did so only long enough to ring the doorbell and run, or to light a firecracker and toss it up on the porch, which just about caused Mister Simmy to suffer heart failure. He did not calm down all night even when she cuddled him in a blanket on her lap and peeled a banana for him.

Of course, that was right after Albert died, at the beginning of all the neighborhood stories. Rommy herself remembered being a child and fearing an old country woman who glared at children from her window. That woman was rumored to be a witch. Folks said that if you looked directly into her eyes, you would die an early and tragic death. Children need something like that to fear. It is good for them. It teaches them to be cautious; it teaches them that in a world such as this they have to always be careful. How strange that Rommy had grown up to become such a woman, an object lesson in fear. When she got tired of trying to win the neighborhood over with offerings of fruit and flowers, she decided she would simply give them what they wanted. They wanted something to be afraid of? She could sit there and be that. After all, she was afraid herself.

Some children liked to taunt the monkey and Rommy committed their little faces to memory in case something bad should ever happen. After all, Mister Simmy was now her only living relative. Rommy had learned, as a very young woman, that she couldn't have children of her own. By now they might have found a way, so much has been learned about the body, but back then it was just no. The slamming of a door. The pulling of a shade. She and Albert talked about adopting, but somehow it never happened. She pictured them eating under the grape arbor with two little ones, a boy and a girl. Albert would pull wonderful strips of colored cloth from his ear and Mister Simmy would sing "Red River Valley" and shoot his little cap pistol.

That's what she thought about while Albert meditated. All of her meditations starred Albert. She wasn't certain she showed up at all in his. He loved her, she knew he did, but in a different, more complicated way. He said, "Love me, love my monkey," and she had. She loved Mister Simmy. She was the one who read all the books about monkeys; she was the one who had told Albert the spider monkey had the most dexterous prehensile tail of all New World monkeys. She demonstrated by having Simmy pick up cherries with his tail and put them in her hand; then she told him to hang by his tail from the clothesline, and he did.

"And you ask why I love you?" Albert said. "I ask why you love me." She did not look at him, just reached and held onto the sleeve of his shirt while Simmy scurried from tree to tree. The yard was teeming with life—bees and frogs and birds—the fruit trees were in full flower and the fragrance of her gardenias and magnolias left her light-headed. It was one of those clear moments of honest recognition, as sure as the blossoms would turn to fruit, as sure as autumn would come around again. She loved him more than anything on earth. She wanted to say she couldn't imagine *not* loving him, but the words were slow coming and by the time she was ready, Simmy was dashing after a neighbor's cat, and Albert raced to retrieve him. Now, she wishes she had said it.

SHE COULD TELL that some of the children were shocked when they finally saw her. They were surprised that she wore shorts and sneakers, surprised that she sometimes yanked her hair up into a ponytail at the back of her head. She had just turned fifty-three and could have been a schoolteacher or a friend's grandmother or a woman working the register at Food Lion.

But people will blame a woman for a man's unhappiness and that's what they did with Rommy. She suspected people said she was not pretty enough, not sexy enough, not local enough (though she had grown up only a couple of hours away). Anyone with an IQ only slightly higher than Mister Simmy's should know better. Rommy knew better herself but it didn't ease the shame and hurt, especially late at night when there was no one for her to talk to other than a chattering little monkey who liked to pick at her scalp. She knew this grooming was Simmy's greatest show of affection —other than offering her food he had already been chewing—so she never scolded him for it. Instead she took to wearing one of Albert's old caps (he often imitated the salesman in *Caps for Sale* for children and had twenty or more in all colors) as they sat there watching the television. Sometimes Simmy fell asleep in her lap, and in just the blue gray glow from the set, someone peeping in from the outside might have thought she had a baby there.

She knew better. She knew the source of Albert's sadness, and even though he knew that she knew, it was never discussed. The folks in town who really knew who Albert was would not be talking. Their knowledge came from sharing the same desires. And she knew who they were. She saw them in the grocery store with their families or featured prominently in the newspaper. She had seen them other times as well; she had seen them creeping out from under her grapevines late at night. Many nights she had heard a car parked over near the all-night pharmacy turn its engine over and drive away, just before Albert tiptoed into their room and eased into bed beside her. If she spoke to him on these occasions it was to pretend that his getting into bed had been what woke her. But usually she kept her breath even, her eyes closed. There were many nights when he stroked her head, his hand gentle as he fingered her neck and shoulders. She knew he loved her. But she also knew if she had opened her eyes to look into his she would have seen a look of hopelessness.

WHEN ALBERT DIED, she felt washed up on shore by an ocean of tragedy. It was Albert's big black wave that came rolling and rolling, threatening to pull her into its undertow and down to the depths forever. It was what kept him making promises that he would never be able to keep. Babies and arbors and trips to the Caribbean. Romantic nights with just the two of them and not even Simmy around to interrupt. But she had understood almost from the first that Albert's plans—spoken with hope and the best intentions—didn't mean anything, just night talk. Come daybreak, all the plans receded.

When Albert died the wave was cresting. Though he tried to keep himself afloat, his mood had gotten deeper and darker than she had ever known it. It still hung over her now. She wanted to crash herself, to give up, too. Instead, she took to gardening as she never had before. She spent hours down on her knees, twisting and pulling weeds from the earth. She spread manure, intoxicated by the rich odor of decay. Sometimes, when the sky was clear and the breeze just right, she would answer Albert as she should have that now-lost day. "I love *you*, I love *you*," her spade striking the earth in rhythm with the words.

If she could have, she would have poisoned Albert's demons, deflated the black doom that shadowed him and their house, found a way to tell him that they didn't have to continue living as husband and wife. That they could live as friends, have separate rooms, that even if a perfect specimen of a man fell madly in love with her, he would have to creep to her bed in the dark of night so as not to betray her real love. *Only Simmy will know,* she should have said. She should have laughed.

• • •

ROMMY'S TREMBLING MOST often set in as she sat on the porch talking to Mister Simmy. Sometimes it was all she could do to get inside the house and slam the door before the hard shaking started. She shook all over. Her teeth rattled. Her bones ached. Maybe she should have let those children see her shake. Let them see her fall completely apart. She overheard someone at Albert's funeral remark that she hadn't done a lot of crying. Was there some prescribed amount of crying for a widow? Folks didn't know that her crying had come and gone early in the marriage and that by the funeral she'd used it up. Folks didn't know there were several men in town who should have been shedding *their* tears at the graveside. Their failure to appear was evidence that their souls did not run to the same depth as Albert's. It had been Albert's desire for an honest life that killed him. Before he died, she liked imagining that Albert might get himself another chance someday, that he might eventually find peace and acceptance, that he would no longer need a good woman to hide behind.

ROMMY MET ALBERT when she was well into her twenties and still living in the town where she had grown up. The smell and sound of the ocean were important to her day. She was waitressing at a seaside restaurant where Albert happened to come eat one night. He was with a big rowdy table of men, all of them drinking beer and telling jokes. He was by far the best looking of the lot and all the waitresses were talking about him. It surprised everybody that Rommy was the one he had fixed on by the end of the night. She remembered feeling like an amazon next to him, too large, too plain. She was one of those girls people said had an *interesting* face, the same people who remarked about her intelligence and love of science, neither of which had ever won her a man's attentions. Still, Albert kept coming back, always meeting up with the same group, always talking with her while he waited for them. They talked about what kind of fish people were catching off the pier and about the erosion of the shoreline. She was working for a conservation group to raise money for planting sea oats and depositing sandbags, and he made a contribution every time he was in the restaurant. He made her laugh as he pulled quarter after quarter, sometimes a rolled up dollar, from behind her ear and let his hand brush her neck each time.

He made people feel good about themselves. He worked magic—magic you could see and magic you couldn't. Soon enough, she didn't care if people wondered why he was with her. She thought she knew the answer. She was stable and cheerful. She *was* smart and she knew things Albert was interested in hearing about: birds and plants, the weather, the stars. He liked the fact that she read all the time and had been to college for two years. But perhaps most important, she shared his love for animals and was always eager to visit a zoo or watch *Wild Kingdom* on television.

They were just married and settling into what had been Albert's family home when there was a terrible accident on their corner. A boy from a nearby town was thrown from his car and speared on a neighbor's fence. Rommy was in her yard when it happened; she was squatting, tending the fragile delphiniums she was determined to grow though it was clear they didn't like the southern climate. At the sound of the crash, she got to her feet and ran out into the street. She was the first one there, but there was not a sound from the boy, only the spit and spray of a busted radiator, the slow leak of a punctured tire. The whole world seemed to have gone silent. The birds had stopped singing the way they do when a snake slithers his way through the garden. For Rommy, seeing death for the first time was dark and silent. She could almost taste the loss as she stepped back at the sound of sirens.

It was the same way when she stood alone on her porch long after the ambulance took Albert away. Her gaze was locked on her neighbor's house, a house that had changed hands many times. Now its yard was cluttered with the paraphernalia of children, but the murderous fence was still there. She felt that if she stood there long enough she might see that boy again. She might watch his death as if it had just happened, as if she had not been thirty and just beginning to learn all that she would come to know about gardening.

ACROSS THE STREET from Rommy's house was the town's sole apartment complex. Gardenview Apartments, it was called. "I think our garden is their view," Albert had said as they watched the units spring up like bean sprouts, nothing but a series of soon-to-be-run-down little two-bit dwellings each with just enough of a concrete stoop to hold a cheap yard chair and a trash can. Many of the children who tormented Simmy lived in Gardenview and were, to Rommy, like scampering cockroaches; their running and jumping and shouting sent Mister Simmy practically into convulsions every time the school bus wheezed to a stop. Once they were on the bus, she had hours of peace in the shade of her own yard. She watched the women of Gardenview. They were almost all military wives, their shaven-headed husbands up and gone before dawn and their children needing attention. She observed their lives, aching with loss at the sight of khaki pants and dingy white T-shirts strung over lines. She watched the women, several swollen with babies, sitting out on their little stoops while children in dirty diapers stumbled about. She often heard them talking and laughing, and though she knew that these were women with very little means, scrimping and pinching just to get by, she envied their lives.

Her longings held even when families split up and moved in different directions, or when the men came home from drinking ready to pick a fight. Come Friday night, who needed television? Who needed some shoot-'em-up detective or cowboy show when she could hear all the cussing and fighting she could ever want to hear sitting right there on her porch. There were more peaceful scenes, too, but they were quiet and not nearly as noticeable—a couple strolling along the sidewalk; a father sweeping his child up off the ground and into his arms; a mother stepping onto the stoop in a fashionable dress, price tags still attached, to twirl for her children and a neighbor. Those were the moments, little promises, that could enable a person to go on living.

THE ONLY OTHER story in town that could hope to compete with the ones the children made up about her (that she killed her husband, that she tortured children she caught stealing fruit, that once a year she killed and ate the brain of a monkey and bought a replacement) was the town's murder-suicide story of 1967. Somehow, though, your story was more sympathetic if your husband killed you first and then killed himself. Everybody had heard it described in great detail: brains on the ceiling, lung on the door. No surprise that the murder-suicide house stayed empty for many years. Apparently nobody wanted the house even after it was gutted and rebuilt and repainted. Through all the years, it had been empty more than occupied. People said the house gave off bad vibrations that over time were unbearable.

People also knew Albert's story, how he used the sash from her silk bathrobe—a lovely pale ivory raw silk—and how he tied it off too short.

SHE'D BEEN IN the yard watering her peonies. It was early morning, a sunny June morning, and she had had the hose nozzle turned to the finest mist of spray so as not to harm the bright saucer-sized blooms. She was picking the ants from the petals; she had leaned close and breathed in the sweet heady fragrance.

Kick gasp kick. The coroner guessed for five minutes.

Now she could hear him. Now she knew. But then she had been hearing a bird far off near the river. She had heard the children from the apartments across the way, calling "The mosquito truck is coming, the mosquito truck."

"I guess he was what you'd call an amateur," she'd said to the coroner.

"What?"

"You know, in the entertainment business," she said, but really she was thinking in the self-hanging business, in the noose-tying business, in the leaving-a-wife-all-alone-to-fend-for-herself business.

"But wonder why he used this," he asked and shook the silk belt from her robe, "instead of this?" He held out the coil of rope that he said was down by the chair Albert had kicked out from under himself.

"Maybe he didn't want burns on his neck," she'd suggested, but what she'd decided to believe was that using her sash was his way of letting her know he was thinking of her at that very moment. He was thinking of the Christmas morning when they sat sipping coffee before the sun rose. He was sending a message to her: *I am thinking of you, Rommy. I cannot put it into words because I can't be sure that you would be the one to read them. I believe you already know all that there is to know and that you have kindly looked the other way. You made a sacrifice and now it is my turn. Because I love you. Because it is your turn to have a life.*

Someday, when she died, would they come in and fumigate *her* house? Would nobody would want to buy it? Would they call it the suicide house and would it stay on the market until some unsuspecting soul from out of town fell in love with her trees and gardens?

ONE DAY IN early fall, she was surprised to see a band of kids on bikes circling closer and closer to her house. She knew they had their eyes on the ripened pomegranates that hung near the ground. She pretended not to notice them and carried on a loud and lively conversation with Mister Simmy. She told the story of Persephone and how the poor darling was left to live in Hades six months of the year just because she ate some pomegranate seeds. Simmy screeched and carried on as he always did when children were in the vicinity.

"What's that?" she asked the monkey. "Did I hear you say that we have company?" She walked to the end of her porch where several had parked their bikes and were crouched down in the dirt. They froze when they saw her there, a circle of dirty faces. She looked around, all the hands slipping into pockets and behind their backs. There were five of them gathered there. One boy was too old and smug looking to be playing with the little ones.

"I'm glad you stopped to pick pomegranates. I have trouble getting down that low," she said.

The smallest girl began to cry and was comforted by one of the older ones, a girl about nine or ten years old, who stood up tall. The girl's dark hair was slicked back in a ponytail and she put her hands on her hips as she stared at Rommy, took a deep breath and stepped forward, dragging the little one along with her. "Are you going to report us to the police?"

"No," Rommy said. "I just want to warn you that the juice stains from a pomegranate will never come out of your clothes so be careful." Her hands were shaking and she clasped them behind her back. "Stain your skin, too."

"Thank you," the tall girl said. She stared directly into Rommy's eyes, then shook her head in embarrassment when the little one cried louder and harder about how she didn't want to live in Rommy's house in a rusty monkey cage. She didn't want to see the dead man in the freezer. She didn't want her tongue put through a meat grinder.

"Can we go now?" the girl asked. "My sister is a little bit upset." It was clear that she was comfortable in her skin, bright and dependable, the kind of girl Rommy had been. "I told her that none of those stories are true but, you know," the girl shrugged, "she's just a kid."

"Here's a story that's true," the older boy said and popped up the front tire of his bike. "Old women who live all alone

sometimes get robbed at night. Sometimes they get *raped*,"
he stretched the word out in such a frightening way that the
little girl buried her head in the stomach of the older girl and
the other two little ones ran toward the complex, leaving
their bikes behind.

"Really?" Rommy shook her head. "That's shocking and
sad. I feel sorry for whoever is so lost to the world that he'd
do such a thing."

"We find condoms out behind your house all the time,"
the boy said. She recognized him. She had seen him spit a
wad of chewing tobacco into Mister Simmy's cage and then
run off behind the apartments. She had seen him tease
Simmy with a banana, yanking it away at the last minute.
He stepped closer, an apple in one hand, as he eyed Simmy's
cage. "People go out in your backyard late at night and do
things you can't even imagine."

"Oh, I *can* imagine," she said. "There is so much activity
of a sexual nature in my yard you just wouldn't believe it.
Some plants, like those pomegranates, have to mate in order
to bear fruit. That kiwi vine, too. Just like in human life, you
need a male and a female in order to produce. And then
there are those lilies whose loud colors scream out that they
want to be fertilized right that second." She breathed out and
unclasped her hands. "And the modest little yucca who

closes up once the process has taken place." The children were watching her, waiting. "Sometimes all you need is a good breeze," she whispered. The leaves were turning and soon they would cover the ground. This year she would get out and rake just as she and Albert had always done. She wished she could hire some of the children to help her. She would teach them all about her yard. They would love that, love gathering apples and pears for preserves to spoon onto piping-hot biscuits. She could have all kinds of goodies ready just as the school bus stopped at the corner.

"May we?" the girl asked again. "May we go now?"

"Of course," Rommy said and they were gone; the boy raced off on his bike and the two girls crossed the cluttered yard of the apartment complex. They stopped and sat down on one of the concrete stoops that looked just like all the others.

She walked around to her side yard and began picking the pomegranates that were ready. They were best when they began to split open all by themselves, the thick skin cracking so that you could reach in and pull it apart, two perfect halves of shiny red seeds protected by the thin white skin that held them in place. She had seen many people in town try to match her fruits; they had even come with shovels to dig up the little offshoots that sprang up in the neighboring yard. Most didn't know what she had just taught the children, that the bushes had to have a mate. She filled the bag until it was almost too heavy for her to lift, balanced some pears and apples on top, and she made her way across the street to the stoop where the two girls had been sitting. She could hear a television going inside. She could smell something frying, bacon maybe. There wasn't a bell so she knocked on the screen door and then stepped back and put the bag down on the stoop.

"Yes?" A woman was at the door. She looked too young to be a mother, too young to be smoking but there she was with a cigarette in the corner of her mouth and a baby on her hip wearing just a diaper. "Can I help you?"

"I'm your neighbor." Rommy pointed over at her house and watched as the two girls came and stood behind their mother. "I brought your girls some fruit from my yard."

"Well that's nice of you," the woman said and pushed open the door. She didn't invite Rommy in; instead she motioned for the girls to go out on the stoop. There was a man in the next room, stripped down to an undershirt and shorts while he painted the walls a pale yellow. He was barefooted. His young muscled arm rolled fresh paint over the dingy walls. "You'll have to pardon me not asking you in," she said. "We're painting and it's a mess."

"Of course." Rommy waited for the mother to go back inside and then she turned to the girls. "Here's some fruit," she said. "You are welcome to come and pick more any time you like."

They looked up at her in complete surprise. "I'd just appreciate your letting me know when you come for a visit." She didn't give them time to say or ask her anything. Instead she turned and made her way back across the yard to her own porch where Mister Simmy was waiting for her. He would be ready to have his dinner and get settled in for the night. He would jump with joy to see her.

Snakes

I WAS GOING to get my tubes tied but I decided to go
to the movies instead. The secretary at the OB-GYN office
kept calling and leaving messages on my answering machine. "Are you okay? Did you forget us?" She sounded anx-
ious; she had lots of loose ends to tie up. Mine were not
going to be some of them. I was okay when they called it
tubal ligation—the tying of the tubes. I do a lot of macramé
and crocheting and so the notion of tying something didn't
bother me in the slightest. It was when I began thinking
the word *sterilization* that I got cold feet. It sounded so
final.

So, I went to see a movie called *Mrs. Brown* instead, and
though I'm not usually one who is into the British royalty

(other than the kind of cheap gossip you might get on the front of the tabloids), this movie really appealed to me. I highly recommend it. My favorite part was watching these Victorian women swimming in full garb, bustles and petticoats and thick stockings.

Now that's the way to keep the cellulite under wraps, literally, not to mention the benefits of sun protection. I ate popcorn and Milk Duds and thought about designing swimsuits for those who don't want to show anything at all—merwomen: timeless, mystical, camouflaged—but the wearers would look elegant nonetheless with their loose white gowns and pale translucent skin. I am far better at teaching high school biology than I am at sewing even though about once a year I buy bolts of fabric and all kinds of patterns that I spread over the living-room floor. Will is tired of my ideas because he knows that as soon as I have cut out the fragile pattern pieces and pinned them in place I'll lose interest or it will be time for my students to turn in their leaf collections, and I'll have to pay hundreds of dollars to a woman I know who does sew, only to wind up with an array of weird clothes that I will never wear. Will has asked that I try not to get any ideas other than those related to my own field. He forgets that I had the idea of the water bra long before there was a water bra. *And* that new device that allows camping women to pee standing up. We could be millionaires if I had ever had an investor, but by the time I get to this part in the conversation, he is long gone.

Every New Year's Will asks me to promise that I will not buy any fabric or crafty, project-related things. His request always follows mine—that he stop playing a game he calls the death pool, where you guess who is going to die during the next year. He has been listing the Queen Mother and Bob Hope for the past six years; I don't even remember who else he said last year because I blocked it out. I don't believe in joking about the dead. Every time he gets on this track I have to knock on wood. Our other annual tradition takes place in summer while the kids are at camp—one night swept clean of all responsibilities and duties. We begin planning it as soon as we hug and kiss Janie and Ben good-bye and watch them get herded off with all the other ten and nine year olds, respectively. We can't imagine that they will both make it the whole two weeks. We anticipate poison ivy and bee stings, broken limbs, near-drowning episodes. We worry about practical jokes and cruelty within the cabin; we fear black widow spiders lurking in the latrines, ticks raining from the pine trees, snakes coiled under rowboats. It was potential danger that brought us together in the first place— two acquaintances who chose to share a cab rather than use public transportation after a late-night party held by mutual friends in D.C.

Now WE ARE in the backyard of a house that is one-tenth paid for—the coals are dying, the dog is gnawing a T-bone. This is our favorite night of the year. We turn off the phone, we drink a little bit too much, and we write out our grievances of the past year, read and then burn them. There were those awful years when everything was very serious and personal—what we refer to as the Dark Ages. Those were the years when our grievances were about each other; they were long and typed and angry and pathetic. The Dark Ages. If you can survive them it will make a marriage much stronger. You just have to get to the other side of the cave and re-enter the world of light and warmth. Sometimes you have to sacrifice a person or two who listened and knew too much, but creatures of advanced intelligence should understand this. If your Dark Ages become the Ice Age, you're having a long weary journey and the meltdown hits you like a blowtorch the minute your children leave home. Sometimes the break is too severe to ever mend. Then all that's left are your sad hieroglyphics in an abandoned cave, an explanation of what went wrong.

If you never experience any of this, then probably you are

living on the surface and will have to come back in the next life as something like a newt or tadpole to improve your status. Or that's what Will thinks. That's what we say to make ourselves feel better, and it works like a charm. We choose the analogy, since Will is a swimming coach, that a marriage that never takes a dive is like skimming the surface of life. You might zip right along but it's shallow, the journey of a simple water bug. We believe sooner or later you have to suit up and dive to the bottom. It's only down there that you can appreciate the light on the surface.

We are relieved to have made it through with only a few scars. During the grievance sessions of the Dark Ages, I typed: "Do you need to go to husband school? Do you need to have your hearing checked? Do you have a learning disability?" I was looking for explanations everywhere. The women's magazines suggested that if I made myself more available sexually everything would be hunky-dory. Seems to me, I'd heard that song before. Like back before the lightbulb. A pop-psychology book said I must first understand his mother and the first months of his life, when he was totally dependent on her. Darwin said that marriage was not the natural state anyway, that the family unit only came about so that the males who needed to be out hunting for food would not fight over sex. And the Bible said—well, forget *that* one.

Clearly there was a common theme emerging. The descent of man.

He was descending all right, and I have never been angrier. I descended, too. My cuspids grew, the fur on my neck stood up. I was afraid to look in a mirror.

That same year, he typed: "You are a bitch."

I wanted depth and details. Why was I a bitch? What kind of bitch? When did he first begin to think of me as a bitch? A bitch compared to who? Didn't he think that he contributed to the bitch factor?

He could not offer a better example, he said, than the one I offered every time I opened my mouth.

It makes me feel sick and shaky all over just to recall. Now, three years out of the cave, I am elated when at the last minute I just grab some little Post-it notes and jot down my grievances. I write "Charlton Heston." I write "nosey friends." Then I write "cellulite" and I am about to write "yeast infections" when I think I better write the confession that I didn't get myself spayed or tied or put out of commission. Then Barbara walks in; she is *the* nosey friend I had in mind.

Now first of all, Barbara *knows* that this is our quiet night at home and that I have been planning it ever since I packed the kids' footlockers and hauled them up to Camp Skyuka.

She is the very reason we have to turn the phone off. But here she is, more hyper than usual even with no apology for busting in.

"Tried and tried to call," she says and flips her hair back from her shoulder. If she does this gesture once she does it forty times. Her hair is black with a streak of gray in the front like Lily Munster or a skunk. Someone in a salon in Charlotte told her it looked sophisticated that way and she believed it. I once counted her doing the hair flip thirty-two times over dinner. Will counted thirty-four.

"Thought you must have been on the Internet." We shake our heads. I glance at the little Post-its on my lap. Will has note cards and I can see he has written "prayer in school" as his first grievance. I am always worried that he will turn our night into a major political rally so I am relieved to also see that he has written "toe fungus" and "swimmer's ear" and "old men in Speedos."

"Oh," Barbara says with perfect fake pity. "Is this your little night all alone? Am I interrupting you?"

Will makes no comment and I—against my better judgment— tell her that it's okay. We just finished eating. I have not had enough to drink to be blunt. This is a grievance I write down right in front of her: "I have trouble being rude even when circumstances merit it."

She would be rude. She is one of those women who really has little interest in other women unless they can be of assistance to her. She would never, for example, join with the sisterhood. She is a man's woman, the kind who would have no problem sleeping with whoever gave her the green light. Her subjects are herself and her family and she reiterates details of those topics a minimum of two times and usually three. Will and I take bets on this, five bucks a hit. He says she does triples most often and I say doubles. When Will is correct, he does his hand like he's opening a cash register and goes *"ka-ching, ka-ching."*

Barbara keeps looking at her watch as if she's about to go somewhere but then she doesn't. She talks about her kids, her Ellen, who is mature beyond her years, and Matthew and Paul, who recognize the brutality of contact sports like football and have chosen to play the clarinet and French horn. As if one means you can't do the other. I want to laugh every time she says Matthew and Paul, because I want to ask where Mark and Luke and John and all the other New Testament dudes are, but I pour myself a glass of wine instead.

"Paul says, 'Mom, the clarinet is my weapon of choice.'" She flips her hair, nails flashing sparkly red in the glow of the citronella candle. "He says, 'Mom, the clarinet. Weapon of choice.'" She grins great big at Will and motions that she would love some wine. "'Clarinet. Weapon of choice.'"

"*Ka Ching, Ka Ching,*" Will says. He scribbles a grievance but I can't read it.

"Three on a match," I say.

"What?" Barbara is jumpy tonight which means she is probably about to ask a big favor of me. Will I go have a root canal for her? Will I sit by her side and listen to her for the rest of my life? Will I give her my husband, who she is constantly asking to talk to about his work and how *can* she improve the muscles of her upper arms—could he ever help her put together a workout program?

"Three on a match. Bad luck." I hold my hand out to the side for Will to refill my glass. I make a face to let him know how pissed off I am getting. "First guy in the trenches strikes a match and lights his smoke, passes it to the next guy, who passes it to the next guy, which has given the enemy time to become alert, aim, fire."

"Where did that come from?" She laughs. "You remind me of Ellen's opera teacher, who is always changing the subject."

"Opera?" Will asks and if I could I'd kick him.

"A fabulous program," she says. "I don't know if your kids are the least bit inclined toward the arts but it's a . . ."

"Fabulous program," I say. "*Ka-ching, ka-ching.*"

"What?" She puts her legs out on the chaise like she plans to stay awhile.

"Where is Ed?" Will asks.

"Who knows," she waves her hand. "First he said he had to work late; then he tells me that he's planning a hunting trip at five o'clock in the morning with some of his partners." She looks at me with her look that says *you know what I mean.* She tells me often that she is convinced that Ed is having an affair. She has been convinced of this for many years. It is what has given her "permission" to have the affairs that she has had, details of which I have pleaded bloody murder not to hear. And there have been many affairs and not very discriminating ones if you ask me. But then, of course, she sees herself as the victim.

"You should have told him to stop by, you know, since you're here." Will looks at me and smiles slightly. Now we're in cahoots. We are a couple. We are beyond the Dark Ages; we are evolved. I have told him everything, even how Barbara once said that she hated Ed so much that she wished he'd die. Even telling such a thing made me want to knock wood and cross myself even though I'm not Catholic.

"Yeah, why are you here anyway?" I ask. "I mean, you and Ed could have a romantic night all to yourselves."

"Well yes, that's true." Then she is silent.

Here she is. Miss Water Bug, who for whatever reason decided way back to attach herself to me and never let go, to wrap and choke like kudzu or wisteria gone awry. She's a cobra, an octopus. She has suckers beneath those nails. She is a parasite ready to hop on any host that passes by. She is a snake slithering into the strike zone.

As I said, Barbara talks only about herself and her family and how everything affects them; this alone would be enough to drive the sanest and nicest person to lock the door and buy a Doberman. Barbara would have driven Jesus to distraction.

"You all go ahead with whatever you were doing," she says. "I just want to relax a minute before I go home and face all the work that I have. I need a wife!" She laughs. "That's what I'm forever telling Ed, 'I need a wife.'"

"You've got a live-in," I say.

"Yes, but what I really need is a wife," she says again. "Not a housekeeper, a wife. But you all go right ahead with what you're doing. I'm not even listening."

"Five bucks to you, baby," I say and Will comes out of a deep thought to do his *ka-chings*.

"We were doing television theme songs," I say. "We have dedicated this evening to our favorite television programs and we are going to discuss them fully and at great length. Then we're going to sing songs from the seventies."

"Oh, you are so funny," Barbara says. "Did I tell you what Ed and I are planning for Ellen's sweet-sixteen party?"

Will starts whistling the background music to *Mister Ed*, which I guess immediately, but it doesn't make her shut up. I say, "Gee, Wilbur," and I snort like a horse.

"We have rented one of the big rooms at the Marriott. Ed knows a deejay who is agreeing to handle everything. Leave it to Ed to know a deejay. Ed, knows a deejay. Who would ever guess that? Ellen said, 'Dad, he's such a hotty. That deejay is a hotty. Who knew?'"

What I know is that she'd leave Ed in a flat second if she could; but then she'd have to work so of course that will never happen. "Who knows this?" I ask and I do the music from *Maverick*, which is very hard for Will because he didn't grow up with the Westerns the way I did. I do *Big Valley* and *Rawhide* and *Gunsmoke* and *Branded*. I go for *F Troop* and *Hogan's Heroes*, and we keep going without a break because Barbara can't play and I love how it feels to exclude her—Miss Opera—Miss Piccolo—Miss Get a Life Why Don't You? She keeps trying to go back to Ellen and Matthew and Paul, but we don't let her. We talk about the *Beverly Hillbillies*.

"You watched that?"

"We still do," I say. "Nick at Nite. TV Land. We have the video of the one where Granny thinks a kangaroo is a giant jackrabbit."

Will says that Jethro has come out and is building a casino in Las Vegas. Also, Jethro is Jewish. Who knew that? I look at Barbara and I say "Who knew that Jethro was Jewish? Who knew that his dad was a famous prizefighter."

"Who cares?" Barbara asks. "Even my children don't watch things like that."

"How sad," I say. "Poor things." And then I do my hand like Thing from the *Addams Family*, beckoning Will, until he does the theme song complete with background music. We act like Barbara is really deficient for having never heard of Uncle Fester or Lurch.

"It's never too late to learn," I tell her before continuing the litany of television trivia. Mr. Brady died of AIDS. Darrin number two of prostate cancer. Darrin number one, who I read was quite the philanthropist, died of emphysema. Bob Denver, aka Maynard G. Krebs and Gilligan, got busted for pot. And years ago there was that urban legend that he died when a radio fell into his bath and electrocuted him. False. Perry Mason/Raymond Burr was gay, which would have just killed my grandmother. *I Dream of Jeannie* married a real estate agent and still looks great. Poor Tony Nelson (in real life, Larry Hagman, son of Peter Pan, aka Mary Martin) needed a new liver *after* becoming J.R. and getting shot. Bob Crane really did die, though. Murder in a Phoenix hotel room. Poor Hogan. They say he was far right of center before he turned to wild sexcapades. Those most rigid and far to the right are always the ones who fall hardest. Jerry Falwell for example. Jim Bakker. Barbara's husband, Ed.

Barbara is getting fidgety. She wants to talk about what she read in the *New Yorker* or the *New Republic*, which we could do but we choose not to. It's our party; our home turf. I say, "When in Rome." Now she has to choose between us and a husband she despises. Every time she tries to interject with Ed this and Ed that, I try to catch her eye to remind her that I know better. But she doesn't look me in the eye; to make eye contact would be a threat to her whole world. Instead she concentrates on Will; she wants to talk about when he swam butterfly in college. She wants to talk pecs and abs and the muscles of her calves.

I tell how Will loved Barbara Eden. He found Mary Ann and Ginger (especially Ginger) attactive, but Barbara Eden was love at first sight. He wanted to live down in that little genie bottle with her. So did I. I wanted to *be* Jeannie. This is the kind of mutual desire (not unlike severe neurosis) that can hold a relationship together.

"Must have been because her name was Barbara," Barbara says and pauses with eyebrows raised to get Will's attention. I watch eyes and brows and foreheads because I read this is where the truth is revealed. The mouth is nothing but a decoy, nature's distraction from the soul. I say, "Oh, are you still here?" We laugh and laugh. Will opens another bottle of wine.

"No, I think it was her belly button," I say. *"No offense, Barbara."*

I tell how my first crush ever was on Dick Van Dyke. I loved him as Rob Petrie and I loved him as Bert in *Mary Poppins*. I loved everything about him. "He still looks good," I say.

"Oh please," Barbara says, so I turn so that I'm not facing her at all. I say, "Dick Van Dyke is the best. That man is still the best." *Ka-ching, ka-ching, ka-ching.*

I AM STILL holding my little stack of grievances—the lovely bottle of chardonnay I had bought for this ritual is gone, as is a cheaper bottle washed down behind it. She has ruined the night. We like to follow the grievances by listing all of the good things in our life. We want to talk about our children, our home, our life, where we will go on the next family vacation. But none of that is in Barbara's repertoire. She has reminded Will about an outing that took place about this time four years ago, something about a hike and a picnic down near Crescent Lake. He remembers, nodding his head slowly until I say that I don't, and then he's not quite so sure.

"It was really such a blissful perfect day; talk about the *best*," Barbara says and something in the night—the breeze, Will's silence, the siren of an ambulance out on the highway—makes the hair on my neck stand up.

"Really?" I ask, but I am not looking at her for the answer. I know the answer. What I tell them is that I know all the lyrics to any Carole King or Cat Stevens song they can name. I know Todd Rundgren and Boz Scaggs, the Doobie Brothers, Seals and Crofts, and Loggins and Messina. I know Elton John and Kiki Dee. I can do Steppenwolf's "Magic Carpet Ride" complete with motorcycle sounds, though technically that's late-sixties but how in the hell would Barbara know that?

There is the pop of a firecracker in the woods behind our house, which brings Barbara up and out of her chair. "Neighborhood kids," I say. "They're practicing for the Fourth of July."

"Isn't that against the law?" she asks, and after humming a few bars of "I Fought the Law," I say, "Your point is?" I hold my stare and she has to look away so I let her off the hook, talk about how when I was a kid, we always went to South Carolina and stocked up on firecrackers and sparklers and Roman candles, which were legal there, and hoarded them until the night of the Fourth. "Haven't you ever broken a law of some kind?" I ask and turn to Will.

"What?" His face is hidden in the darkness, the dwindling coals barely illuminating the shape of his body.

"You know," I say, Barbara's eyes wide and alert. "Haven't you ever done something dishonest?" I stand and walk over to stoke the coals. A Roman candle soars up above the pines with a whistle and a pop. "Sky rockets in flight," I sing, but Will doesn't join in on this awful seventies tune. He can't remember the words.

"I always hated that song," I say. "How did it ever make it to number one?" I look at Barbara and wait like she might have the answer. I look at my watch and marvel at how late it is. "And what about 'I've Been to Paradise but I've Never Been to Me.' How did that song make it? Who listened to that?" I motion for Barbara to rise like I might be the pastor about to deliver the benediction. "Ed is going to be so worried about you," I say. "It's really late. It's like 'Midnight at the Oasis.' 'It's too late, baby, now it's too late.'" Barbara tries to join in and sing along but she doesn't know the tune or the words. She looks at her watch. "Oh my, it is late. I bet even Ed might be home by now." She puts her cheek to mine and air kisses. "I left his dinner in the microwave. Delicious veal Parmesan. That's what I need." She makes lips to cheek contact with Will.

"Veal?" I ask. "A woman to fix your dinner?"

"No, I need to go home," she says and laughs. "I'm so glad that you all were just sitting around. It's great to have the kind of friends you can just drop in on." She flips her hair and jingles her keys. "I don't see enough of you two, lately." We stand and watch her slither down the drive, and then I sing, "Bye, bye, Miss American pie." I sing, "Evil Woman," "Witchy Woman," "The Bitch Is Back."

We wait until her car door slams and we hear her back up and drive down the street. "So much for the evening as planned," I say. "Pre-empted by *As Barbara Turns*, the worst soap opera to ever run. She sees more than enough of us, don't you think?

He says, "Oh yeah," and laughs but his back is to me as he picks up the bottles and empty plates. We promise each other a rain date. We can try again tomorrow if we don't get a call from camp that someone needs stitches or wet the bed or broke a neck.

We hit the cool clean sheets and I turn out the light. I tell him that my biggest confession (which usually follows grievances) was that I went to the movies instead of getting my tubes tied. He says that he lied earlier today when I asked him to buy salmon steaks for dinner and he came home with T-bones and a story about how the seafood cooler wasn't working and he was afraid to buy spoiled fish. He reminds me that James Garner, aka Bret Maverick and Jim Rockford, another of my favorite men, used to advertise beef, and I remind him that was before the triple bypass. We laugh and then lie there listening to the last sputters of fireworks.

"That's the worst you can do?" I ask. "Would you swear to the god of *I Dream of Jeannie*? Would you vow to never again watch television if you're lying, not even for special events like presidential debates or assassinations or moon landings?" I reach and turn on the lamp over the bed and in that one startled second I see more truth than I wanted. And in that one second, I have to weigh out the good and the bad, the past and the present. I have to think about how easily lives can be poisoned and pulled apart, even those that shouldn't be.

"So," I finally say. "There are worse things in life."

"Such as?"

"Transitions. Not knowing what is coming next." I laugh. "Like if I were in purgatory, I'd beg to go to hell just to get it over with."

"Yeah, me too. What else?"

"Cannibalism. Serial murdering. Having to eat olive loaf and pickled eggs while wearing a Qiana jumpsuit and watching reruns of *Diff'rent Strokes*.

"Or losing what you care about the most."

"That, too."

Now A FULL year later, we prepare to burn our grievances again. Joe DiMaggio is dead—lungs. And the Lone Ranger—heart. The second Mrs. Kravitz from *Bewitched*—stroke; and poor Allen Funt—*smile, it's* Candid Camera—stroke. Grandma Walton and Mr. Gianelli from *Bob Newhart*—lungs; and Iron Eyes Cody, the crying Indian from the KEEP AMERICA BEAUTIFUL commercial. Dr. McCoy from *Star Trek* and Peggy Cass *To Tell the Truth*. Gene Rayburn from the *Match Game*—heart. And Ed is dead— stroke—something no one was expecting. Another victim of excessive living.

• • •

BARBARA HASN'T COME around much since then and I suspect it's because I know too much. I know that she had long wished Ed would die so everything would be easy for her—a large inheritance and an empty bed. I know that she was ready and willing to turn on me if and when it served her purpose. She might even think that I have begged every detail of her slipping from her skintight pants as a means of punishing and humiliating my mate. But Will and I are more evolved than that, which is what I practice saying in case she ever brings it all up. *We have legs to stand on*, I say, *we have spines*.

Tonight, content with visions of our children armed with flashlights and bug spray, I take out my piece of paper and write: "the Dark Ages; natural disasters; fallout." I hold it while Will strikes the match. We are celebrating one more year away from the pull of darkness. We are celebrating honesty. And as we do all of this, we are more vulnerable than ever before. Our planet is one orbit closer to the sun that will eventually consume it. Our lives are one year closer to the end. And though we are grateful and relieved that we still have each other, there in the dwindling light of the fire, we are aware that somewhere someone is dying. Someone within minutes of where we are sitting lies dying on this average summer night.

Turtles

EVERYBODY ON THE east hall at Turtle Bay Nursing Home spends most of the day in the television room. There is nowhere else to go. No doors to outside are left unlocked or unattended. If you want to look at the creatures out in the marshland behind the home (they say big turtles come up and sun themselves all the year round) you have to go to the cafeteria and press your nose up against the glass, which the people who work in there don't seem to like at all. Carly tells them *she* doesn't like the fact that the only big window near her room is made of stained glass and it gives her a dark sad feeling to try and see through it. Jesus is standing in the window with a flock of sheep and it makes her really uncomfortable to press her face up against the robed leg of Jesus in hopes of seeing some old snapping turtle that would love nothing better than to bite your hand off.

"I've yet to see a turtle of any kind," Carly tells them. "The brochure made it sound like there was a constant show. The brochure made it sound like someone like me—a little old, a little arthritic, a little hard of hearing and seeing—could have the time of her life."

"You can, baby," one of the women says and pats her hand. She is a large woman, a few too many biscuits for sure, hair too dark for her age, but she has a kind face. Not all of them do. "Just not here right before the supper hour when we're so busy."

"Are there any turtles living out there in that filthy water?" Carly asks. "Or are they kind of like my son, who *almost* appears from time to time."

"Oh yeah, I've seen a few," the woman says and leads her back over to the door where, if you can believe it, a line is already forming. Carly skips dinner often and this night is no different. They'll come looking for her but there's a good chance they won't find her until it's bedtime, and if she's lucky, one of the nicer ones will offer to fix her a sandwich. If not, she has a stash of candy under her mattress.

Here at Turtle Bay there's no separation between those

who are perfectly sane and those who are demented. You might live across the hall from somebody who still gets up and drinks coffee and reads the newspaper (like her friend Betty), or you might have a neighbor who doesn't know who she is or where she is and just spends the day washing her hands and toweling them dry or pacing the hall. That last describes Carly's neighbors. She has a wanderer on either side of her.

Here they put the focus on the legs and hands. If you are ambulatory (this includes wheelchairs and walkers) and can feed yourself, you can stay on the east hall even if you can't remember who you are. The way to remember which wing is which is easy enough though: East means you can still rise. West means you are left setting.

If you are an invalid you get sent to the west hall even if you have every particle of your mind intact. It's sad to wander over there and see them all hooked up to machinery, no choice but to wear those diapers like big bedridden babies. Even Homer, the big shaggy mutt who lives here—the latest in pet therapy—is not allowed on the west hall, which is sad for those old souls who would love nothing better than to stare into Homer's kindhearted brown eyes. Carly figures they are afraid that Homer might mess up the equipment.

He might accidentally unplug somebody with his tail, and then where would the poor creature go? Court? Tried for manslaughter? Sent to the chair? Carly worked at the Fulton County Courthouse for forty long years and she knows just about everything there is to know about the law.

On the east hall there are those who walk all day long and then they walk all night long and still they never get where they're going. There's one that's blind and she still keeps walking, tap tap tapping that annoying cane. If Carly wasn't the type to feel guilty for doing unkindnesses to others, she'd trip the old fool and hope a hip might break and land her in the west.

Now that Carly Morgan's whole life is behind her and she is just sitting around waiting to die, she only has two favorite things—other than her son, of course—left in the world. Well, three if you count Court TV, but seeing as how it is rare for her to get to watch something smart, something other than *Wheel of Fortune*, she sticks to two favorites. The first is Homer, the dog who without a doubt loves her the best out of everybody and would sleep right there on the rug by her bed if that one ugly night nurse would stop stealing him. The second favorite thing is Mr. Wilton White (Whitey to those close to him) who has not lived at Turtle Bay long.

He keeps his distance from most everybody. He says he wishes Dr. Kevorkian would stop by just once—that's all it would take—that it's unkind the way that humans are forced to cling and linger. He believes that a man should be able to do what all animals know is the best thing to do—crawl off alone and die in peace.

The nurse says, "Let's not be so gloomy. You are among people who care."

He says that he is in this hellhole as a last resort; he says that's what the name of the place should be—the Last Resort. His wife died over fifteen years ago and he says that nothing has come even close to being good since. *Since me, that is,* Carly knows that's what he is thinking. One night she got up and crept over to his room. Homer whined and carried on from where she'd tied him to the leg of her dresser while she stood watching Wilton White sleep. He was so handsome she couldn't believe it. She needed to lean in close to hear his breathing, to rub her cheek against his stubble, to press her mouth against his. It scared him good when he opened his eyes and saw her there. He was so frightened he almost rang for somebody but then when he realized it was just Carly—his neighbor and confidante, his secret lover and soul mate—he didn't. He did talk to her in a serious way, though. He told her how when *Elizabeth* (that's the wife)—when *Elizabeth* died he had to turn out all the lights in his home and watch television in a darkened hallway. He said if word got out to the widow patrol that he was home, then they would all start arriving with pies and symphony tickets.

"And you don't like pies a bit," she said. She could tell at first meeting that he was a layer cake kind of man. She could tell he needed somebody like her. "And the symphony, shoot." She knew immediately where he was coming from. He is not a bit boring.

Carly has finally, after a lifetime of waiting, after a husband who left her to raise their boy alone, a boy who has grown up to be so successful that he doesn't have time to visit, after her other relationship that went on for over twenty years, a secret relationship that left her all alone on the weekends and holidays, after all that, she has finally found her true mate.

It was while she was over in his room that the nurse went creeping in and stole Homer. She wishes he'd bite that fat rear end, but maybe not—if Homer took to biting on a regular basis they might have to get rid of him and that would break her heart. Homer loves Carly. You can just look at his sweet face and know it.

THERE ARE SOME people in Turtle Bay who can't shut up and that is the truth. "Diarrhea of the mouth and constipation of the brain," Carly says. She loves that little saying. She used to say that (to herself, of course) years ago at her job at the courthouse, where she was a receptionist for four decades. The favorite receptionist. She had to listen to those poor folks who were trying to get some unemployment. You have never heard such. And you have never *seen* such. The lawyers, young and old, handsome and ugly alike, were always impressed by Carly and her fund of knowledge, the way she did everything just right, and they told her so regularly. They couldn't believe that she herself had not thought of going over to some place like Wake Forest and getting herself a JD. And Whitey was a lawyer for years and years right over there in Greenville. He even remembered being in the Fulton County Courthouse. She might very well have greeted him and directed him to the correct chamber; she was probably too in love at the time to even notice such a handsome man. Fate. That's what Carly calls fate.

That one big nighttime nurse is a real puzzle. The residents don't know what *it* is. One of the women from the west hall—the one who is forever wanting to show what is under her Ace bandage, which of course nobody wants to see, looked up and said, "Is you a *him* or a *her?*" Carly and several others leaned in close to hear the answer but then somebody on *Wheel of Fortune* won a prize and there was so much screaming she didn't hear what the answer was.

Late one night, Betty—she is the smartest one here next to Carly and Wilton White, JD—said, "Let's set fire to his/her britches and then watch and see what kind of equipment is under them big saggy drawers." Of course, Betty is also hatching out a plan to go ahead and kill the nurse because it keeps stealing Homer from where he stays by Carly's bed and also stealing Betty's candy bars, even though Betty has said over a million times that many a diabetic has to eat sweets from time to time and that she is one of this particular kind of diabetic. Betty said, "If you don't believe me, you can read it in a medical journal." Betty's husband had been a doctor—an arthritis doctor—so she tends to know a lot about medical things. She has terrible arthritis herself and thinks now that her husband is dead and buried that he might have used her for some of his scientific research, injected her with some bugs that ate out her joints or something.

Betty says she also knows all about the homosexual conditions. She says she once knew a nice man who got the devil beat out of him for being that way. "My husband always believed that the homosexuals was just like animals when it came to *doing things*," Betty says. "He said those people were like cats and dogs when it came to fighting over who might get some loving." She pauses to make sure Carly gets what she means like she might be a simpleton, and Whitey stops reading his paper—fine print, too much for Carly to handle on the average day—and he asks, "Who is?"

"You know who," Betty hisses like a snake and nods her head in the direction of him/her. "The homosexual ones."

"Nonsense," Whitey says, his face getting red and that cute vein that runs across his forehead popping up. The nurse is always fussing over how poor Carly's veins are and so she'll have to remember to point out Whitey's to show him off. That will make him feel good. "Good veins," she says and grins at him. She just loves when he voices his intellect. He gets to leave Turtle Bay on a regular basis and so he knows a lot about what is happening out there. He has a daughter from one town over who comes and takes him for weekends. "Thank God," Carly heard him say once when he saw the daughter's car pull up. Carly usually waits at the front door with him. One, because she loves to be near him and two, because residents are only allowed to have cigarettes outdoors under the watchful eye of one of the guards.

Carly never even smoked and has only taken it up so she can get outside and enjoy the fresh air from time to time. Betty is a real smoker; she's been at it for sixty-five years. She says that she has special immunities to cancer. The *it* nurse lights their cigarettes for them, so Betty had the idea that they should talk about women things when the *it* is around and see if they can guess by the reaction. Does *it* nod in agreement when Betty tells of going in for a "Dustin' and a Cleanin'" (DNC for those who like the scientific terms, Betty says) or when Betty tells (at too much length) about when she had her hysterectomy. Betty whispers in a harsh voice for Carly to join in but this is a hard topic for her to discuss. These are private matters so she sits there with her arms crossed over her chest, ridges of scar tissue left behind there from her surgery. She was not immune to cancer. She also knew that her days of meeting her true love in the darkened parking lot over near the courthouse were long over. She was only forty-two. Her boy was in high school, concentrating hard so he could go to college. He was ashamed that his daddy had left without a trace and now he was ashamed that this had happened to her. So was she. She felt it was some message from the great beyond that loving a man who already had himself a wife and some children was wrong. This was her punishment. What man would want to look upon her barren chest?

WHITEY'S DAUGHTER IS beautiful and his little grandbaby has long golden hair that Carly just has to reach for and wrap up in her hand. She says "pretty pretty" like a little lullaby until Whitey takes to shaking all over and he says "damnit woman." He is showing off for his daughter, letting her know that Carly is his woman. She follows them to the tall wire gate of the porch, the nurse holding onto the nape of her sweater, and his sweet daughter keeps turning Carly back with a gentle push, telling her good-bye. Carly says, "Take me, please take me, too," but the daughter says, "I'm sorry, really I am," and Whitey is shaking all over by now. He says, "You have got to make another arrangement." Sometimes his speech is garbled sounding but Carly hears this clear as a bell, and his girl says, "I'm trying, Daddy, I'm trying." He is all the time talking about *his arrangement* but what about *her* arrangement? What about the way that Carly is left to live? What about her son? If Dennis would just come see her, they could walk outside and look for the turtles; she would remind him of his pet turtle she got him one Christmas. He named the turtle Slowpoke and it lived in a little plastic paradise complete with a set of stairs and a beach umbrella.

A son is a son till he takes a wife but a daughter's a daughter all of her life. Carly wishes now that she had a daughter; she wishes she had his daughter and she closes her eyes and imagines that it is her strapped there in the car beside her. The girl says, *Oh Mother, I've missed you so.*

"Please," Whitey says as they drive off, and Carly thinks he might be crying. He is worried about her, left there all by herself even though she has tried again and again to reassure him that she has been alone most of her life. She took care of her parents until they died and then she took care of her husband, a man who never really loved her. If he had, he would've stayed; he would have tried to make her life a better one, and he would've given the boy what he needed to grow to be a good man.

Carly is temporary here at Turtle Bay, too, just like Whitey. And she meant to tell Whitey's daughter this bit of news but by then they were driving away. She watched them disappear and then she walked back up to sit with Betty in a little square of sunshine. Carly is the most ambulatory of them all. Everybody compliments her on this and says what a good job she does. She gives the Nike shoes a lot of credit and Velcro is a miracle; for a woman with fingers that aren't as nimble as they used to be, Velcro is a godsend. Whitey would be more ambulatory if the stroke hadn't left half of him weak. But he can still make it up with a walker and a cane and that's what keeps him here in the east.

BETTY IS BACK on the story of how she came upon her husband, Darnell, face down in his garden—heat stroke. Carly has heard this story ten million times but she is the only person on Betty's intelligence level so she listens again. "I turned him over, there in the garden," Betty is saying and kind of acting it out like she always does. "His face was so white it shocked me. White and cold. I knew he was dead but still I threw myself there atop him. Oh my, when you love the deceased you'd be surprised what you'll do." Carly doesn't dare ask what she means. She is still distracted by hearing the word "white" like Wilton White. She stands and walks to the gate, that nurse right on her heels calling her back. She presses her face against the fence to see if he has come back so fast. "Who just said, 'Mr. White'?" she asks. "They said, "A call for Mr. White: line two.'"

"You don't listen," Betty says. "Nobody listens."

"I listen," Carly says. The nurse reassures her that there was no announcement made for a call. After a few minutes of watching the empty road she comes back to her seat.

"Honey, don't I know just what you mean. I know it all clear as day."

"You've loved a deceased?" Betty asks and Carly can tell she's getting a little jealous, just like she gets jealous when Homer lets Carly hold tight to his collar instead of her.

"I've loved many deceased," Carly says. She doesn't say that she's thinking of men who might as well have been dead. That she is thinking of herself and all the parts of her life that have slowly died away.

"Hush," Betty says and squints her eyes up in that mean way she does when she starts planning fires and murders, so Carly changes the subject to what she had seen in some of the books over in the television room. She tells her that there are all sorts of different things the young women are inserting into their private region down below and that these things are photographed and right there in the magazines that the men look at as well as the women. This makes Betty laugh and get off the hate track but it also leads her to act like Carly is not as smart as she is. Carly is about to say that she had thought that maybe Betty's precious Darnell was one of them that went after the lovin' like a cat or a dog or a he/she person, but then she decides not to say anything at all because Peg, who has Down's syndrome, has come out there to join them. Betty is the one who taught Carly to say Down's syndrome because her husband used to be a doctor and so Betty knows what is correct even though the rest call Peg a mongoloid. It doesn't seem to bother Peg which you call her if you give her something to eat.

And Carly does. She walks back and forth to the candy machine all day long with a pocketful of dimes that people give her when they come in the door and she says "Good morning. Now how can I help you today?" and she holds out her hand and without fail they will drop something into it. They aren't supposed to give money to Carly, or so the nurse says, but how can they resist when she is sitting there looking so pretty, the best receptionist that they have ever had, and just needing one thin little dime.

"Oh dear, I've just got quarters," Whitey's daughter had said and Carly said, "That's okay," and she took them—five of them—right out of her hand. That got a candy bar for Betty and some Necco wafers for Peg.

BETTY SAYS THAT when they actually do kill the nurse, Carly will be the lookout woman because she is so good on her feet. She will knock real loud as he/she approaches the room. They did a test run not long ago, only

Carly kept thinking it was him/her and knocking when it wasn't. And then sometimes if she concentrated too hard she was able to see people who she just couldn't believe were out here at Turtle Bay. She saw her cousin, Alma, who died from lack of breath when they were kids and then she saw Lawrence Welk, Buster Keaton, and then him, her favorite lawyer in the world—her favorite man in the world—who often complimented her fragrance and asked why nobody had latched onto her yet.

"I suppose I've not yet met Mr. Right," she said, putting on a few airs to let him know that she could communicate with the brightest and the best. She was already thirty-five but no one ever would have guessed.

"Oh but you will," he said and stepped up close behind her. When she glanced down his suit jacket fell forward alongside her hips, that's how close he was standing there, and she could feel his body leaning into her backside, a slight hard pressure against the base of her spine. "I'm sure you will."

And then every day he found a reason to step there behind her at the counter. He might reach up and over her for a file out of the top drawer or he might stand right over her as she bent to retrieve a paper clip and upon looking up, feel his warm large hand cupping her face, the crease of his fine wool trousers brushing against her flaming cheek. Thomas Fenster, JD. Thomas Fenster with the thick dark hair and monogrammed cuff links, the one often shown in photographs in the town paper for various social activities and good causes. The one who made sure that the poor children from across the river had a way to walk to school other than over the train tracks. The first man in the whole town to have a pool in his backyard, and there he was, pushing against her every day, begging to meet her some late night after work when they could do all of the things he knew she wanted to do.

They would go for a little ride. He had a son just a year younger than her boy. That thought alone should have stopped her, but it didn't, and what began one lonely night stretched on and on.

Now IT IS late and she is waiting out in the hall to carry off the plan. The he/she is making its rounds. Whitey still hasn't returned. Homer is tied to the end of her bed with the cord from her bathrobe. He can't wait for her to come in and snuggle up to him. She is about to decide that she's going to go on to bed and forget about the plan when she sees him again, Thomas Fenster, down the hall. He looks so young. He hasn't changed a bit. She waits to see if his wife or any of his children are with him, but no, he is all alone. He will try to unbutton her blouse like he does every single time. He says that nothing will change the way that he feels about her but she doesn't believe him. She fears that the sight of her chest might, even though she goes to great lengths to find bras that cover and fill her out. He has not seen her naked chest in years and years.

"Where have you been?" she asks and runs out into the hallway. "I've been waiting here for hours." And he looks surprised like she might not have a life other than coming at his beck and call. Like it is no big deal for her to sit in a parked car in a dark lot waiting for him to finish eating his dinner and kiss his children good night. She is sure he kisses his wife and tells her he hopes he won't be too late, if he can just finish all this paperwork, they will have a wonderful restful weekend. And meanwhile she sits there when she ought to be home with her own son; it makes her feel sick to imagine him sitting at the kitchen table and working so hard on his homework while thinking that she is at a meeting at the church. She is ashamed of herself but still can't find the strength she needs to drive away from it all. She crouches down so as not to be seen by people passing by.

"I thought you were dead," she says. "They had a funeral and everything."

"Stop it," Betty screams. "Stop it right now." Betty rolls her wheelchair out from behind the door where she has been sitting with a big ginger jar lamp cradled on her lap. They had sat up late one night to decide that this was the weapon of choice: heavy enough to knock out the nurse, thick and round enough that Betty doesn't need what the physical therapist calls fine motor skills to pick it up. "Who are you talking to? The dog?"

"I saw Thomas," Carly whispers. "He's back and I don't know what I'll tell Whitey."

"You're lying," Betty screams. "You tell the same crazy story a hundred times a day, now shut up!" She looks like a witch, her lips smeared over with fuchsia lipstick and her brows filled in with black crayon like a clown. "They're going to send you to the other side if you don't quit. They are. I don't care if you can walk, they're going to take you. They'll tie your hands and feet to the bed and stick a tube up your peehole."

Betty goes on and on, building up an anger until she has a kind of seizure that leaves her out of breath and blank looking so Carly doesn't say a word when she sees Gracie Allen, who has always been a favorite. She's such a card. If Carly could choose to be somebody else that's who she'd choose and she tells her so as she passes. She says, "You always look good. Pretty as can be," and Gracie says, "Why thank you, dear," and then Carly says, "You have always been a favorite of mine," and Gracie stops and takes Carly's hand in hers. Gracie smells wonderful. She smells like Carly imagines a Hollywood mansion might smell. "You're sweet," Gracie says and Carly watches her move on down the hall. Why she is going to visit the old blind man who thinks he's still in the marines Carly can't say. Maybe Gracie has come as part of the USO show.

"Is he/she coming?" Betty screams in slow syllables like Carly might be the mongoloid. Betty has bounced right back and has that lamp clutched up to her chest.

"Not yet." But the Dorsey brothers are out in the parking lot and so is Petie Wagner, who Carly loved in the tenth grade. That was her last year of schooling and one teacher pushed for her to get a kind of diploma that would tell what she had done. People in the country just didn't have time to go to school forever and ever. Besides everybody knew that her family was smart aplenty without school. Thomas knew it. He was pressing against her back right that minute even though his wife was on line two. His wife was nothing more than a red light blinking at that moment and for many moments after, days, weeks, months, years. How could that have happened?

"Now?" Betty calls but Carly has to stop watching for a minute. It's hard to see. Instead she looks out through the dark robe of Jesus and watches the driveway for the car lights that will bring Whitey back. The church across the street has a sign lit up that says ESCAPE THE HEAT, NOW AND ETERNALLY. Lord yes. She is picturing herself in a cool cool place like the creek where she used to swim, like the cool leather luxury of Thomas's Cadillac when they parked at the far edge of the parking lot and he explained how much he loved her even though his position in town didn't allow him to leave his marriage, how he would love to help her with her boy's expenses but his wife would be suspicious, even more than she already was; he was kissing her neck, slowly unbuttoning her blouse, his fine motor skills perfectly tuned when all of a sudden she hears Betty screeching and crying out. She is so mad, cussing and carrying on. The nurse comes in and sees Betty sitting there with the heavy lamp raised, and if the cord hadn't looped and twisted around the back of the wheelchair, she would have done some real damage. As it was, the lamp slipped from her hands and crashed down beside her chair, the body of it shattering into hundreds of pieces. He/she snatches the 3 Musketeers bar that Carly had just bought and slipped in Betty's pocket as a surprise. The nurse says, "That's it, the last straw, *you could have killed me.*" He/she says Betty is going straight to the west hall, which, when all is said and done, probably means that they think Betty is failing fast.

"You let me down," Betty screams at Carly. "I hate you. I hate you. I wish you were dead."

Hours later and Carly can still hear her. *Whore. Home wrecker. How could you do this to me?* She still hears Betty even though she and Homer have been sitting here shaking and crying for nearly an hour while they wait for *Wheel of Fortune* and while Carly waits for Whitey to return.

Days pass it seems and when she asks where her boy-friend, the lawyer, has gone, she is told home. He has moved back home, back where he belongs. He is lucky, they say, he has a family. So now Carly is left with only one favorite thing in her life and right now he is struggling to get away from her because that old marine down the hall has taken to bribing him away from her with treats. A boy's head can get turned quick by what he decides he wants in his life, and of course, what he doesn't want. He whines and pulls but she will not let him go, not this time. This time she is staying there with him all the night through. She buries her face in his pretty brown hair and whispers what a good boy he is. "Please forgive me," she cries. "I'd go back and do it all different if I could. You know I love you better than life itself, don't you? Don't you see that I always have?"

Starlings

AT TEN IN the morning the temperature has already hit a hundred degrees and the weather station says it will keep rising. Mary squints out at the thermometer. The glare from the tin roof of her porch is making everything in the yard wavy. The big oak tree that was already big when she was just a little girl trying to climb up its rough trunk quivers limply overhead. She remembers squashing her face into the bark as she grabbed the branches and pulled herself up. But that was back when the only thing beyond her yard was a couple of houses down the road and the flat tobacco fields, the strip of woods that kept that old snake-infested river shady and cool. That was back before the interstate plowed through town, taking away the fields and the woods and bringing with it all kinds of businesses and crime.

Now she is seventy-six and it is the hottest summer that she can recall, every summer of her life spent here in this very house, though now everything is overgrown and changed. Now the downtown area has spread in every direction and she lives on the corner of what is considered an old black neighborhood. Now her road is paved and the area is overrun with college students who want to live within walking distance of the campus, where Mary spent the last good years of her life working. She swept and mopped and cleaned up somebody else's garbage, somebody that knows better or ought to, given what their folks pay for them to sit and spraddle their long legs out, toes of dirty sneakers marking up the walls. Retirement. Hah.

She has worked every day of her grown life. She has worked in dry cleaning, breathing steam and chemicals, feeling the folds of her lungs starching and stiffening. She has kept other people's babies, changed their dirty diapers and whispered love words when the young mama is out somewhere in a business suit, trying to look like she might be somebody. They say, "Oh Mary, how we love her." They say, "She is like family." This is what they want to believe to be true. Sometimes she wants their lousy wish to be true as well, but then there'll come a moment of reckoning that sends the skin of her neck up in little points. A rabbit running across her grave. She don't want to be somebody's charity. Don't you go doing your good deeding on me.

But now she wishes she'd let that young college boy from next door help her get that air conditioner out of its huge carton by her front door. He said, "I can put it in the window for you," and his thin white hands trembled when he spoke, like he might be scared of an old wrinkled-up black woman. Like maybe he'd never carried on a conversation with a black woman. Maybe he was taught at an early age to fear darkness. Like she might say *boo* and he'd up and run for the hills like that salesman done the day he come calling where she was setting with some children and he gets a scared look when she glares at him like she might up and slit his puny white throat, with those little children standing there in the doorway in diapers all wide-eyed.

Lord, yes, that's how a child is meant to run. Naked as a jaybird. Squat by a tree or down by the creek. Sprawl your limbs out in a warm patch of grass or over a hardwood floor that's cool. The coolest spot in the house is always right down on the floor, where the cool air seeps up from the dark underneath part of the house. She loved playing down there as a girl. She loved the feel of the cool black dirt and she saw it all from down there. Her mother and the other women who lived down that dusty road being picked up on summer mornings, their white dresses pressed perfect like they might be high-paid nurses heading off to the hospital. But then her mother came home late afternoon smelling like somebody else's little girl while her own little girl had spent the afternoon with the children from nearby who ran wild without any grown-ups telling them what to do. The teenage girl who smoked cigarettes, her stomach already swole up with a baby. The big brother who was known to pin a girl down and rub hisself up against her belly, only giving in to her begging and crying if she lifted up her shirt. Mary had done that, turned her face into the cool black dirt while the whole neighborhood watched, while he called her Tiny Tit and pinched her there. She counted in her head all the while picturing her mother walking the clean padded hallways of a big brick house, the little girl's room with a closet full of Sunday dresses and ruffly blouses that nobody was going to push up off her thin frightened chest.

"I hate that girl you keep," she told her mother that night and on many others before bed, her mama too tired to even tell a bedtime story. "I hate her with her old white face. I hate her for thinking you love her." And then she wanted to ask *Do you love her? Do you?* But her mother just frowned and let out a tired heavy breath. What could she say if she did love that girl and what difference did it make if she didn't?

And Mary hates that skinny witch on the weather channel right now, too, with her flashy red jacket like she might be Miss Patooty. They all the time is wearing bright red and bright blue, strutting their feathers and saying *Look at me, look at me, I'm over here in the television set.* Look at the sky and tell the weather. Lord. She gets it better than most of them on the average day. You ain't got to go to school or wear a suit that costs the same as a automobile to be able to lick your finger and hold it in the air. You ain't got to live in a mansion with a Jacuzzi like all these folks have to be able to see how fast the clouds is moving or to take note of the sunset. People have thrown out common sense and trucked in a bunch of horse mess to make themselves feel great big and important.

THE OAK IS quivering, quivering in the heat, the very movement putting her in mind of the old man who once a year stood at the front of the church and played his violin. That sound made people cry; it was a sad sound. People said he knew it all by ear—that he couldn't read words or music; he just played what his heart felt like playing. It was a lonely sound like that sad bird she hears every morning, calling and calling, hopeless of an answer. Now as she watches the branches in that bright light she feels the same sadness. Beneath the tree is a ring of jonquils her mother planted, the Lord only knows how long ago, and every year they come up, weak green shoots, no blooms. They haven't bloomed in over twenty years.

Once when she was a child, she stared up at the sky on a bright hot day. She searched the uppermost branches of that same old oak tree for a bird she heard calling. A sad sound. She waited and waited. She passed out from the brightness, the whole world growing dark and grainylike, the sounds in the air buzzing like something she could see, something she could reach out and touch. Her father scooped her up then and carried her to the shade of the back porch where her mama was running some sheets through a wringer. She never told them that she had forgotten to breathe while standing there, that the heat and brightness made her feel like a candle melting down into a shapeless puddle.

"LET ME HELP YOU," that white boy said. "I know you live alone here and I don't think you can get the air conditioner in the window by yourself. Please, let me do something for you."

SHE HAD READ stories of young men muscling their
way into old women's houses to rummage their purses and
then rape them to death. It was in the paper all the time.
Poor old woman comes out of the Harris Teeter and gets kid-
napped and what did they want? Her car. Her food. Surely
she'd have given them that if there was no other way.
She'd've said, *Take it, children, take the money and the car keys
and just leave me here in the parking lot and I won't even call the
policeman until you are way out of town.* But it seemed that
killing was a part of the plan. They wanted to kill is all.
Many of them do.

"I can manage," she told that boy and watched him amble
back over to where he lived with a herd of wild ones of all
sizes and shapes and colors. The kids from the university had
been coming and going in and out of that old eyesore of a
house for over twenty years, strewing their beer cans and
talking the same stuff; the only thing that changed was their
hairdos and outfits. That boy looked kind of hurt when he
turned to go back into that zoo of a house but she couldn't
worry on that. Would she have let a black one in? She had to
think it through. But no, she thought, she absolutely would
not. This had nothing to do with color. It had to do with being alone in the world.

• • •

"YOU ARE PREJUDICED, MARY," her coworker Bennie
used to tell her when they took their breaks from cleaning
up the campus buildings. "You are bad prejudiced, girl."

"Maybe. Maybe I am," she said. "Or maybe I'm just jealous
of their clean easy worlds."

"They don't all have clean easy worlds."

"In a town like this one they do."

"So do a lot of the black folks."

Those times there with Bennie were the best part of her
life. Those were the times when all the anger that churned
her insides just up and flew away. It made her want to sing. It
made her want to crack jokes and laugh great big. She liked
to tell jokes that were kind of dirty just to see Bennie get
nervous and have to stare down at his feet while he chuck-
led. "You're something else, Mary," he said and she knew
deep down that he meant that; she knew deep down that he
felt something stirring. It was like the world was humming
then, the great big oak trees there on campus filled with star-
lings, their wings shiny black in the light. People talked of
these birds as a problem, the racket they made, the filth they
dropped, the way they clustered together in one big mass and
then took to the sky all at once: a screeching black cloud
that drowned out everything else on the face of the earth.
"Pests," people cried, like they was one of the Bible plagues,

but Mary liked when they gave her that loud second to catch her breath and turn her attention off of Bennie and what was a hopeless calling. She liked changing the subject after the racket like about how she had ordered herself a radio with a built-in cassette player that could also just play sounds. Like you could have yourself a thunderstorm or the ocean or birds at sunrise just by throwing a switch.

ONE DAY SHE will get everything organized. She likes the catalogs. That is her favorite thing, to sit and choose pretty things and then pick up the phone and call, put on a fancy-sounding voice. It is like being a kid with the Sears and Roebuck's only she's old and she has worked hard enough to save. She owns her house and she gets her pension. Her daddy paid off half the house and then she finished all by herself. Didn't need a man even though there was many who offered. *You think I want to spend my life feeding your fat behind and all those children you've planted in other women's patches over the years? Come here to this garden to rest till the end of your days? Think again, you. Think again, old dog.*

THE ONLY MAN she'd've ever had was Bennie, and as is true with everything good in life, he was spoken for, and his wife was the salt of the earth. Still sometimes when she closed her eyes after long days at the university she pictured herself laying there with Bennie. She'd rub her face up on that Egyptian cotton pillowcase she was so fond of and think of him. This was a pillowcase anybody would be proud to have; it comes from a place that has made bed linens a specialty of sorts. Her sheets are just like those she used to spend hours ironing in a big house on Main Street where she worked a little as a young woman. She loved to iron those fine linens. It was the finest cotton she'd ever run her fingers over. Buttery smooth. When she closes her eyes at night ain't a soul on earth, not the president and whoever, and not Prince Charles and Camelia, or whatever the harlot calls herself, sleeping on a better piece of fabric.

THERE ARE BOXES to unpack and when she pulls out the new things it will give her a burst of energy and she will be able to get busy. It will be like Christmas morning right in the thick of a hot-as-Hades July. She'll put on the sound of a tropical rain forest, and she'll hang herself some new curtains, white priscillas with some beautiful hummingbird tieback holders. Pottery Barn and Crate and Barrel and Ross-Simons and Bloomingdale's. She fancies that they see her name come up on the computer screen and they comment what a good customer she is. *What exquisite taste.* She laughs. If they could see her now. Skinny black woman standing in the kitchen in nothing but underwear, nothing but a pair of size medium cotton drawers from Dillards, her breasts hanging and swinging to and fro like a Watusi. She imagines stepping out on her porch this way next time a white greasy-faced thing comes selling something. She'll put an old chicken bone up in her hair and she'll shoo him off with some mumbo jumbo, leaving him to think she'd cast a spell like she once done somebody at the dry-cleaning store.

That man was hateful like she'd never seen, talking to that skinny little white girl at the counter like she might've been a dog. Mary stepped forward and held out her hands and begun to twitch like she was picking up some kind of wave or something. "What is wrong with you, woman?" he asked and Mary just shook her head. "Oh, I ain't the one with the problem I fear." And she told him—much to the shock of everybody there waiting in line—that she had picked up on his sex problems and she sure was sorry. He acted like she was crazy as a bat but still he pushed her. What did she mean by that? She didn't answer, just went on about her business, but as he was leaving she went over and whispered in his old waxy ear, "Your lovin' days is over, sir. Your equipment is likely to just ride around in your drawers like a little dead varmint for the rest of your days." She was asked to leave soon after but that was fine enough. The other workers looked up to her. She was a legend. Besides, her lungs needed a break from all the chemicals and heat.

AND IT IS SO HOT. Too hot to breathe. The hottest summer in a long while. By noon it is a hundred and five and the woman on the television set says it ain't over yet. Mary has pulled all of the heavy yellowed shades to block the sun and feels her way around the boxes and piles of newspapers. She makes her way over to the crate with the air conditioner and sits on top of it. Order from Sears. Why didn't she let them install it? Was she ashamed for folks to see the un-opened boxes? The trash that needed to be hauled out? The recycling? Or was she scared of him, scared of what he might do to her if she didn't tip him enough cash? Now she can't re-member. She hears that stray cat meowing and scratching on her door. Her feet are swollen or she might ask it in. But the last time she did that it was a spooked cat and left a bloody stripe down her arm. It is odd how dark it is in here. Beyond the shade there are kids blowing their horns and riding their bikes. They are buzzing and screaming.

SHE RAISES THE BLIND. Bees in the clover. A distant knocking. A woodpecker? That boy again? She does not trust such young men. There was once one that let her know she was an animal herself if she had to be. He acted like he wanted her for herself but that wasn't what he wanted at all. What he wanted didn't even need a face or a brain. She could have killed him so easy. She said, "Don't make me kill you." She had a tiny little crochet hook she grabbed from her bedside table—one for making lace—and it was pointed right at his ear. She said, "Don't make me kill you because I will." She said, "I will puncture your brain. Or maybe I'll let you live and go on to prison because old butt-buggering bubba might need hisself a date to the prison prom." She could have killed him, could have beaten the everlovin' life from him. A few things like that happen in life and you stop trusting even when you want to so bad.

By one o'clock the sun is beating full down, pressing the cracked ceilings closer and closer to her face. The old oscillating fan lifts the pages of the catalogs at her feet and she can't keep her eyes open at all. She struggles to stay awake; the next radio show is a gardening show and they have lots of tips that she will need in another week or so when she is feeling better. She has bought herself some half barrels and several big bags of good rich potting soil and a couple of bags of moo doo and great big red geraniums. The porch will be beautiful then and when the heat breaks, she'll put on that

222 • Jill McCorkle

frock she ordered from Bloomingdale's, a frock that nobody would ever expect *her* to wear—bright green jungle print with loud-colored animals turned every which way—and she'll set there in the swing with some iced tea in that pretty crystal goblet from the Ross-Simons set and she will open all her Harry and David goodies, maybe break out the Godiva chocolates she ordered several weeks ago and that caviar she was aching to try out even though she suspected that it was probably going to be a lot like when she got herself lox and bagels. Orange fish on a piece of tough bread. *What was the Jews thinking,* she wondered. "You can have it. Buy yourself some mouthwash, too," she told that old man in the fish market. She said, "What has happened to you, man? This ain't no fish market. Smoked fish and orange fish and ole slimy mess. Where's the catfish? Where's the flounder? Where's the cornbread crumbs to roll it in before you fry it?" He laughed. He wanted to say that's a black thing, a colored thing, a Negro thing, an African American, Afro-American, Kwanzaa-celebrating thing. Kwanzaa is what the white folks latch onto in a town such as this so they can act like they're teaching their children something. Teach them collards. Teach them don't cross the street and hold tight to your purse when you see a black man.

THAT BIRD WITH the sad sound is high in the oak and now Mary knows she has to go and see it for real. She makes her way, naked and dark, heavy bare feet wedged into satin slippers, *the perfect end of the busy day for the woman of the nineties.* She stares one step ahead, the brown painted floor. Who painted it last? Her daddy? That man that tried to take up with her that time? Don't trip. Don't fall. Dark floorboards she used to walk as a child, arms held to the sides and balanced. She was on a plank high above the Pee Dee River. Below her were alligators and above her were snakes swinging from the limbs. And watching her was everybody in the whole town—man and woman and black and white. All the children in her school held their breath as she crossed, her own breath held. *You can do it, Mary,* they say, *You can do it.* In her mind she is always being a hero.

HER DADDY SAID, "Mary, what are you doing?" and he yanked her through the kitchen doorway, her white cotton socks stained brown from the paint. "Didn't I tell you not to walk on that floor? Didn't I tell you?" And his grip on her arm hurt and she shut her eyes and waited for a slap to sting her bare leg. Fly swatter, switch—ligustrum limb stripped of its leaves, a whistle through the air, a slap, a sting, pulling the skin up into a thin welt. She never got a whipping in her life that made her want to be a better person. It was the opposite. It made her want to be a bad person. It made her want to beat them right back. Bennie hisself thought that children who were beaten on would grow up to do the same to theirs unless they got hold of a book or two or talked to a person who might teach them different.

"Bennie, you act like a white man," she told him. "Like one of these teachers packed with brains."

"I act like a man is all," he said and she was thinking, *I wish you did, honey. I wish you did 'cause if you acted like most men, like the men I know, then I'd've had you by now. I'd've had you at least once.*

SHE WANTED HIM. He was the one she wanted. But he was too good for her. The floorboards are straight and narrow and it's hard not to tip to the side. She made herself a promise never to strike a child. Never to hit a loved one. But beyond that any fool is fair game. She ain't one to go hunting but you muscle your way into her life with some bad intentions and she will kill you. She says, "I can kill you. I will. I will kill you if I have to."

She'd done just that before when an old bloodthirsty bulldog belonging to some no-good down the street come into her yard like something from the wild and went after a little puppy belonging to those students next door. That dog walked right up and grabbed that puppy by the throat, broke its little neck, shook it like a dust rag, and that young boy was off on the steps wringing his hands and sobbing. And without thinking Mary got herself an axe and went after it. By then the animal had tore open the little one's belly and was lapping right into it like it might be a bowl of milk and she brought that axe down before the mongrel could think. And yes, it looked at her. And its eyes looked frightened. Its eyes seemed to say *I can't help that I was raised this way. Raised to be angry and mean*, but that didn't stop Mary. And when a full day and night passed and nobody came looking for it, she wrapped its body in some old bath towels and called up the department of sanitation. The boy from next door came back later to say that there was nothing the doctor could do for his puppy. He stood outside her locked screen door, hands in his pockets as he shifted from side to side. "Thank you," he said. "I hope I can help you some time."

OH THAT SAD SAD BIRD. Her daddy should hear it. He should have to hear it. And her mother. The boy from next door, his little bloody puppy wrapped in his nice leather jacket. He should hear it. She could let him help with the air conditioner. He is a grateful boy. He means well. And Bennie, God rest him. She opens the shade but now the bird has moved. It's flown to the rooftop, then up past the hot glint of tin, rising and circling, higher and higher. She cups her hands up to the glass and watches, waits, holding her breath. She holds her breath, the pulse in her temple keeping beat with the kitchen clock that has hung there over the doorway since she was just a child watching the hands turn closer and closer to when her mother would get home. A mother should tend to her own home first. She stretches out on the cool floorboards to wait, pulling deep breaths in and out, in and out. She closes her eyes to the bright glint of the tin roof as she pictures the bird there, circling and swooping. When she can get up, when she is not feeling so tired, she will set up that air conditioner and she will unpack all of her beautiful things. And who would ever believe she had grown up to own such beautiful things? But for now she just needs to rest and wait, to tune her ear to that bird far far away, its wings spread as it lifts and circles the hot tin roof of her porch, circling and calling until others swarm in, filling the sky with darkness.

Fish

WHEN YOU LEARN that you are dying, you take off your glasses and never wear them again. I think that you don't want to see the looks on our faces as we sit here by your bed. I think you want only the blurry outlines of our warm bodies bending and whispering, stroking your face here at the end when they say the senses of touch and hearing are what remain.

The woman who had nursed you when you were a two year old with pneumonia sixty-odd years ago has come to be with you, hold your hand, speak softly about what a fine boy you have always been. We know your story about her and how you've always been sure she was the reason you had survived.

I picture that long-ago scene, you on a little cot in the up-stairs hallway, your siblings in the rooms on either side. Two older brothers in one room. Two older sisters in the other. There had been another child, a stillbirth the year before you were born, and there were stories of deformities and how it was a life that was never meant to be. You said that as a child you thought often how your partner had died and wor-ried that you would share his fate, that your life also was never meant to be. When I picture your childhood bed, your little boy face from old photos, the corner of a house I re-member well though it was torn down a long time ago, I see you, sweaty and shivering, and a young version of this very old woman by your side whispering words of love and kindness.

"Oh honey," she says and then turns away from your bed. We all know that she can't save you this time.

When the doctor told you that you were dying, you paused and then said, "I am sixty-four years old and I have had a good life." You have not mentioned death since, except to say that you will be sorry to miss all the events in the lives of your grandchildren: recitals, ball games, gradua-tions, weddings. Jeannie's son, the oldest at eleven, cannot leave your side; he sits and repeats back to you all the stories you began making up for him when he was barely two. We are surprised that he remembers with such detail, but he doesn't want us to listen. It is a secret he shares with you. You have given each of the grandchildren a secret story or joke at some time or another. They all take turns leaning in to kiss you, to whisper, to make you smile. Now you ask that I hold up the baby. "Hold him way up high," you tell me. "I want to see his whole body."

You were terrified of the water, but you loved to step into it, chest deep, pool edge within reach. This was your metaphor for life. Nearby I dove, an extension of your limbs. I spiraled and flipped and you held your breath and cheered silently, one hand raised in victory, as I paddled my way back to you.

And we fished, hip deep, waves lapping, surf pulling. You warned me about the undertow, the whirlpools, the sting-rays and jellyfish that appeared so benign. And when I caught what we called the toadfish—sharp serrated teeth and spiny jagged gills—you gave up and simply cut the line from the bloody hook wedged too deep within his mouth to reclaim. "Poor old guy," you said as he twisted and flopped against the current. "His girlfriend is going to be so disappointed tonight." You laughed, but I knew from the sadness in your eyes that you understood disappointment better than most.

I asked if he was going to live and you said, "Oh, sure."

"He'll have to stay home from *school*," you said, nudging me with the pun. "But just think of the fishtales he'll have for his chidren and grandchildren. He will always be the one that got away."

ON YOUR LAST DAY, Mom, Jeannie, and I sit by your bed and sing all of your favorite songs: "When You're Smiling," "I Can't Get Started," "Blue Moon." You stare vacantly upward, your eyes dry and frozen. "Blink," we say. "If you can hear us, just blink."

WHEN I WENT off to college you offered advice.

1) If you get a flat, do not stop until you can pull into a well-lit, public place. Drive it on the rim if you have to.

2) When you go to a party (if you have to go to a party), fix your own drink (if you have to have a drink). Guard and protect it the whole while just as you do yourself. An unopened beer is always a good choice.

3) You are never too old to come home and it is never too late to call your parents to come and get you.

AND WHEN I needed to come home, you came to get me. Terrified of flying, you flew, white-knuckled, sweaty. And you worried the whole time we loaded everything I owned—not much—and drove out to the interstate in our rental car. We both smoked then and that's what we did all the way home. We played the radio, gave each other an occasional high five or victory sign, and revved our bodies with enough nicotine to go the whole long distance without stopping for the night. The trunk was crammed with things I had owned most of my life—quilts and books, stuffed animals and a rusty three-speed bike that had not worked right since it had gotten stolen and then returned in college. The backseat was filled with forgotten items, some of the wedding gifts still in their original packing—crystal and china and tiny fancy dishes I had never known what to do with. "We all make mistakes," you said every hour or so. "And you're young," you added. "Your whole life is ahead of you."

And now I'm over forty and soon will give your advice to my own children. I have cans of Fix-A-Flat. I have a jack and a spare, flares, thermal blankets, change for a phone call.

I always lock my doors. I don't get in a car without glancing into the backseat. I do not go shopping at night by myself, even during the holidays when the parking lots are crowded. I only drink beer in the bottle and I know that I am still not too old to call, just that it's not so easy these days.

I'LL TELL YOU something you might not remember. It was during a summer vacation at Ocean Drive. Remember the little white cottage where we stayed on the bottom floor several years in a row? Young boys sold Krispy Kreme doughnuts door-to-door. Our upstairs neighbor greased his old (you weren't even forty then) body in olive oil and whistled "Red Red Robin" so loud and so often that we all began to exist in that rhythm. There were raft rentals and sno-cones, sand and salt. Jeannie said we should write a note and bury it; she was nine and I was five. She said she had to do the writing. The note said: "It is 1963. We are the Miller sisters. We are two kids from Fulton, who are visiting South Carolina and some day when we are very old, we will return to dig this up and remember the day." She said that when we returned we would drive Cadillac convertibles and live in mansions with handsome husbands. I added that we would have lots of fluffy puppies and kittens and she said she wrote that part down, too, though I couldn't be sure because it was in cursive.

But what I remember most is a can of red Play-Doh and how we had barely arrived and unpacked when I rolled and pressed the clay into the braided rug of the rental cottage. It got stuck there, a sticky mess, and I got in trouble. I rubbed ice cubes over the spot, rubbing and pulling every little speck. And isn't it odd? I knew even as I sat there, rubbing and picking, that I would never forget, that I would think of it often. That I would grow up to believe that rectifying a mistake is sometimes reason enough to exist.

YOUR FATHER MADE his living carving up dead barnyard bodies—cows, lambs, pigs. Your child's eye made no connection between those bloody slabs hanging on hooks and the pet goat you kept in your backyard. You may not have connected the red of your father's eyes to repossessed furniture and your mother's sad anger. You only said nice things and we grew up to love him, so much so that I fell in love with a boy who smelled like him only to later realize that the treasured memory I carried of your father was one of straight bourbon and cigarette gone to ash.

When you were late for school, you told the teacher the

goat got loose, that you chased him for blocks on end. This was a teacher you adored, the same teacher who over thirty years later would also teach us, regularly confusing us with Mom, asking with a teasing grin if we were still sweet on you. The goat was your pet. That part was true. But what you really did on those days you hooked school was wander downtown and shoot pool in a dark ancient room where you stood and stared out. Your eyes were always drawn to the light. How frightened you must have been the first time you could not find any light at all. The times your heart was so heavy you could not rise up from the bed. Now if you told your story, others would step forward with their own. Now there are articles and books, more than you could ever read, miraculous medicines that take emotionally paralyzed people and bring them back to life. But not then. Then it seemed you were all alone with your fears and worries. And there were many people willing to let you believe that, to believe that your overwhelming sense of loss and sadness made you less of a man. It changed the way that I looked at a lot of people. Though told to respect my elders, I often did not. It was hard to respect ignorance and harder still to respect those who knew better but still offered nothing.

• • •

YOU MUST HAVE seen us standing there those times, children who were afraid to move too far from where you were, even though it was summer beyond the windows of your bedroom and kids from the neighborhood called our names to come out and play tag or hide and go seek, to mount our bikes and take out after the mosquito truck. How shocking it must have been to look down from your hospital window that time and see us there in our Easter dresses waiting for you to come home. We were too young to visit inside, so you came out into the sunlight still wearing a light blue robe and navy terry cloth slippers. You stayed long enough for us to hug and hold onto you while you repeated how sorry you were, sorry that you had to be there. And after you went back inside the tall brick building, one of the adults told me to count up the windows until I got to the fifth floor, that you said you would be there to watch us drive away. I couldn't see you — the windows were caged and dark — but we waved anyway.

You had bought a card for us in the hospital gift shop and we opened it in the car. It was a happy card with ducks and bunnies and chickens, a card about love and joy and the birth of spring. It made us sad. The only resurrection I cared about was yours.

Animals were my closest friends then: cats, dogs—ours, the neighbors', wild skinny strays that I would offer bits of food in hopes of taming. You loved to talk about animals. Your childhood cat, Smoky Mac, once stuck his head in a jar, ears held back in curiosity as his whiskered nose bumped glass. Then he was alert, ears pricked and raised. And he found he could not get loose. He could not get his breath. He ran like wild, heavy jar tight like a helmet, and you, a boy no older than nine or ten, chased after him. You caught his wild body and pinned him down. You cracked the jar with a rock so he could breathe, and though he hissed and scratched, and though he did not come home until the next day, he knew to be grateful. He sat near you whenever he could. He never scratched you or stuck his head in a jar again.

WHEN YOU COME home from the hospital this time, we know that it is the beginning of the end. We know that you will no longer sleep in your own bed, but in one that is equipped with bars and an IV line, an oxygen tube. We will come to rely on the hospice workers who come and go throughout the day.

When you came home that other time, it felt like life was starting again. You were young and had many years ahead of you. There was hope. Your dad arrived in a taxi and sat quietly with his hat on his lap; he wanted to say things but he didn't know how. In less than a year, he would not be able to say anything at all, a stroke and throat cancer having left him to stare out at the end of his life. On one of those afternoons, I went with you to visit him in the hospital, but again, I was not allowed inside. The adults took turns going in so that someone stayed with me under the huge trees where I fed the squirrels, so fat and friendly that they came and sat right in front of me and begged. I asked you to read to me, and you said that you would, but could we please read something other than *The Little Match Girl*. But that was the one I wanted; I wanted to cry. I liked to cry. It had become a kind of hobby, this need to imagine myself or someone I loved taken away. I had to prepare myself. Even now, I feel that's what I'm doing—every word, every image is a match struck in an attempt to hold on.

On the afternoon you die, we keep asking for a sign, a blink, a twitch. We sing "All of Me," "Today," "Moon River." And when it is finally time, Jeannie and I both know at the same moment. We feel it, a static tension in the air, and we communicate it without words, rushing to get Mom to come in from outside where she has finally agreed to go for a rest, rushing to bring your brother to be by your side.

And when you take your last breath, you blink—one strong blink, and then you are gone.

Now I HAVE DREAMS. One takes place in our old backyard. The swing set casts long-legged shadows toward the house. I pull you up on a swing, tie your arms to the chains to hold you upright. Your head slumps down. You wear the robe of a sick man and I sit beside you, watching and waiting. I am a kid, my hair cropped short, my knees scabbed, my feet bare. My swing creaks back and forth while yours stays perfectly still. And then the people come. A steady stream of strangers passing, looking, nudging, whispering. *You are a sick little girl*, they say. *Sick to sit and hold onto the dead.*

But, I say, *he's not. He is* not *dead.*

Over and over I argue and then dusk comes and all the people go away. It is almost dark and we are all alone and you lift your head and look at me, your eyes a blue gray I had almost forgotten. You wink. Point your finger and wink. *You're right*, you say. *I am not dead.*

YOUR DAD HAD an old collie he called Bruno, a black-and-white creature he walked to the corner store every afternoon. He was retired but he still liked the smell of cold cuts. He liked the way the little market still had a floor covered in sawdust and plenty of bones stashed away for Bruno. This is how I remember your father. Small and neat with a hat he politely tipped at everyone he passed. He held my hand when we crossed the street. His eyes were the same color as yours. This is the man I knew, not the troubled one of your childhood, not the one who stumbled out in front of the bleachers at a high school football game where you sat in the middle of a warm flock of kids, Mom's smooth young hand held firmly in your own. And without a word, you rose to your full height and made your way through the crowd. You never thought to do anything except to carry him home. And if this single act were all I ever knew of you, it would be more than enough.

Now I DREAM you are in the mirror, bathrobe loosely tied, arms outstretched. I know with the strange knowledge dreams allow that you cannot speak. All the energy you can gather is used to shape your image. And one by one we enter the room. And one by one we ask, *Do you see?* In the room there are three of us left to mourn and grieve. In the mirror we are a family of four—a simple image of thousands of days. You sign to us with arms reaching, *You,* and then, hands pressed firmly to your chest, *are my heart.* Hands crisscrossing, a shake of the head. *That's all that there is.*

You actually spoke these very words near the end, when your eyes were still able to blink. Tiny tear, cool saliva. "You are my heart; that's all that there is." And on a later day, nearer the end, your eyes dry and frozen in that distant stare, I leaned in close and whispered, "I'll be looking for you."